CHANGE & OTHER TERRORS

CHANGE & OTHER TERRORS

A COLLECTION OF SHORT HORROR STORIES

JIM HORLOCK

EDITED BY
DAMON BARRET ROE

Change & Other Terrors:
A Collection of Short Horror Stories
by Jim Horlock
Published by Quill & Crow Publishing House
Edited by Damon Barret Roe

Cover Design by Fay Lane

Interior by Cassandra L. Thompson

Printed in the United States of America

ISBN (ebook): 978-1-958228-65-4

ISBN (paperback): 978-1-958228-66-1

Publisher's Website: www.quillandcrowpublishinghouse.com

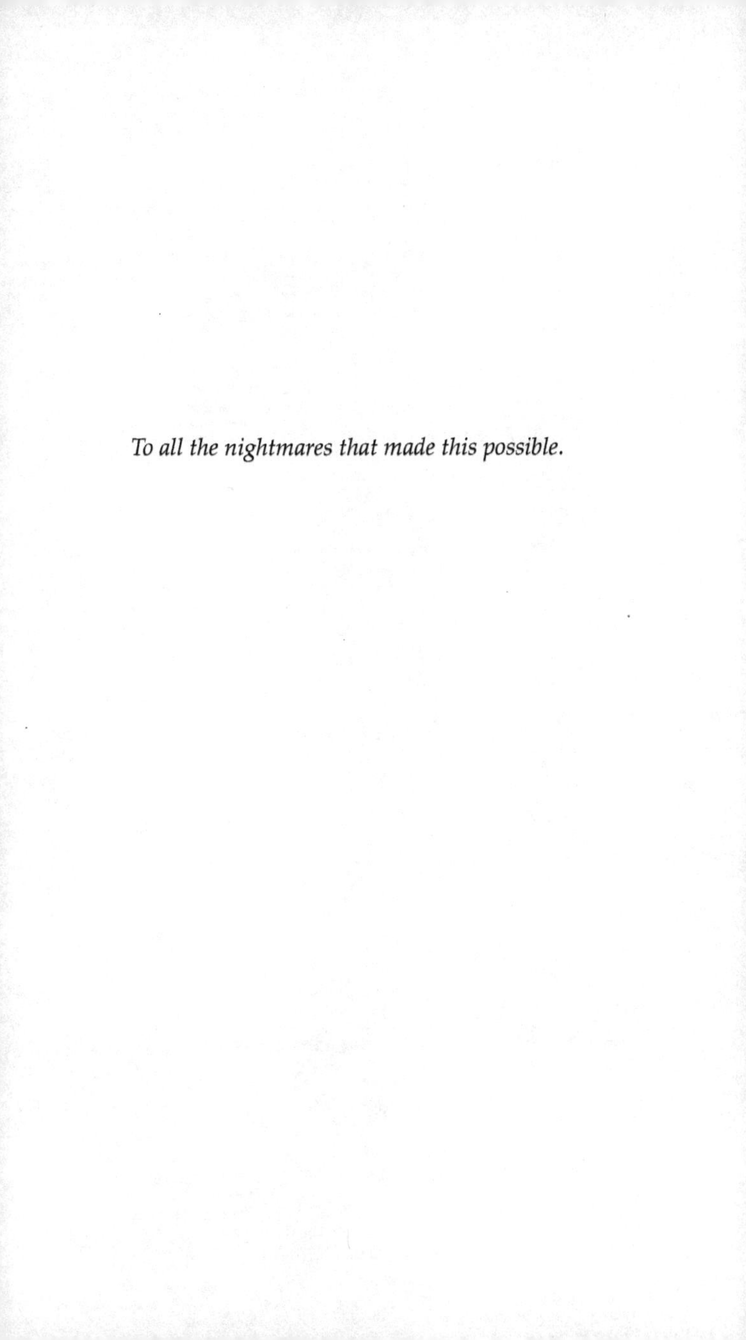

To all the nightmares that made this possible.

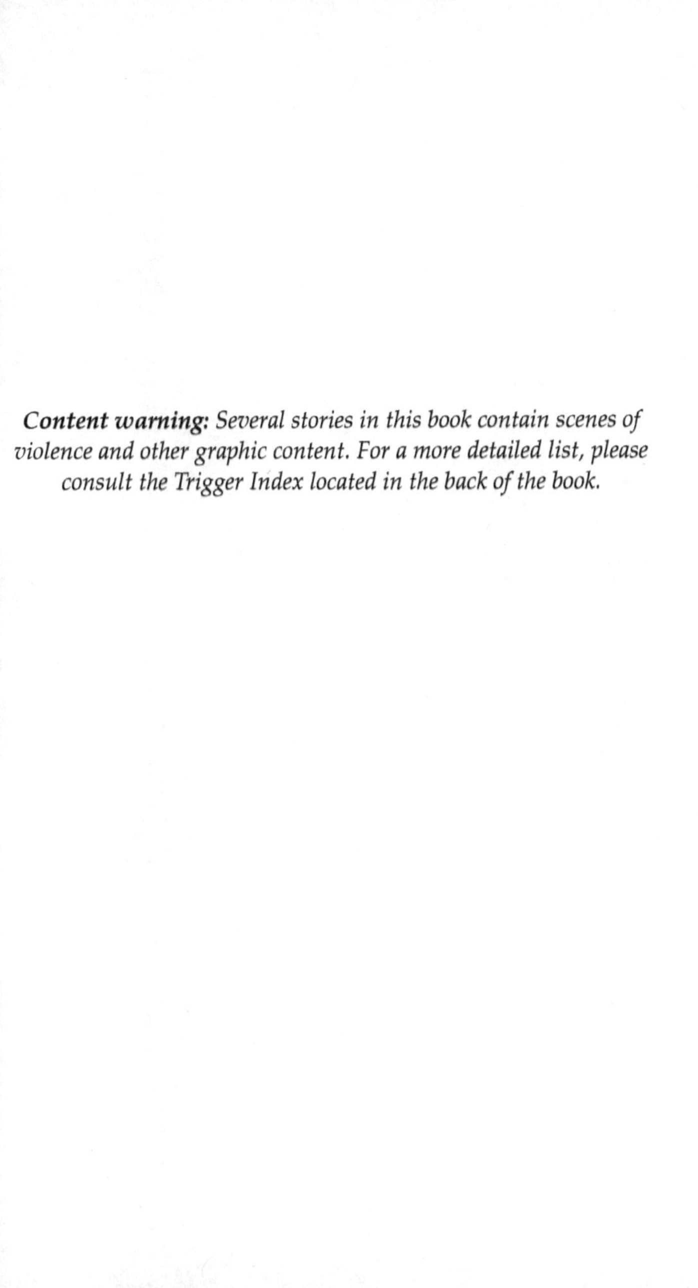

Content warning: *Several stories in this book contain scenes of violence and other graphic content. For a more detailed list, please consult the Trigger Index located in the back of the book.*

INTRODUCTION

JIM HORLOCK

Change might mean a new flavor of crisps or a knife in the ribs, but either way, I hate it.

We all experience change in life; that much is certain. Heartbreaks, new beginnings, bittersweet endings, and fading friendships are things we're all familiar with. Most of us learn to get along just fine with it.

I hate change. I jerk away from it instinctively, the same way I would from sudden intense heat or a large, unexpected spider. I understand that change is integral to the human experience; it's unavoidable and crucial to life, but I can't bring myself to embrace it.

I've written this collection about change almost by accident. The theme knit itself together under the skin of my stories without my notice. At first. It seems natural that when writing about fear, we can't help but put a little of what terrifies us into it.

Many story ideas come to me in nightmares. I get an image, sometimes just a single intense scene, and I can't resist pulling on it like a dangling thread. *Growing* was like that; it all came from that image of Josh on the bed. *Lullaby,* too, with the image of the stroller beneath the streetlight.

Epiphany, on the other hand, was very much constructed with intent. Perhaps the darkest story in this collection, it explores ideas around people suffering for art and that only by experiencing trauma can we find inspiration.

Horror is change. We're all Dr. Jekyll knowing that our Mr. Hyde is fast approaching. The person we will become is not the person we are now, and there is nothing that can be done to prevent it. That's the true horror at the core of this collection. I hope you enjoy it.

- Jim Horlock, 2024

CONTENTS

LIMBS

I hear them all the time.

All day, their noise fills the city. There's no traffic anymore. No noisy engines. Most generators are dead and the grid is down, so there's no constant background hum of electrics. No bustling human crowd either. Sound travels a long way in the quiet.

No matter where I go, no matter what I stuff my ears with, I can't seem to get away from the noise. Howling, gibbering calls that make my brain itch. High-pitched wails and grotesque warbling, made by vocal cords stretched to the maximum and beyond. Or worse—and if there's one thing I've learned since all this started, it's that there's always worse—the ones that still sound human. A little girl lost, screaming for her parents. A mother weeping with broken-hearted sobs. Cries of anger so close to normal that you could almost believe them.

Until you realize that sound is coming from a mouth with too many tongues or a throat longer than your arm.

These sounds are a mirage of water to a man dying of thirst. The promise of hope. The truth is hard and sharp as a knife between the ribs: there aren't any people left here. Every day I'm getting closer to certain that I'm the last one.

There is no hope.

I sight one of them through the scope of my rifle. It can't see me; I've picked out my position on the roof for maximum cover. This one looks damaged like it might have been in a fight, but it's hard to know for sure. I've seen them attack each other before, but not often. It's dragging two of its legs, and it's unsteady on the others, making for a strange, shambling gait. It's leaving a trail of some dark fluid, smears, and spatters on the long-abandoned pavement. Could be blood. Could be some kind of mucus. You can't ever be sure with them. I once saw one that spun webs like a spider. The strands had little bits of bone, chips of teeth, and fingernails stuck in them. Webs made from people it had eaten.

The thing clicks its teeth together mindlessly as it stumbles onwards, and my anger builds, a bottled thunderstorm in my core. Sometimes, it's stronger than others, pressed right against the glass. Sometimes I barely notice it, but it's always there.

They've taken everything from me. *Everything.* The hate at the back of my throat tastes like acid. It crawls up to the bridge of my nose and makes my eyes water. I wonder, how many people has this one killed? What hell did it put them through first?

My finger tightens on the trigger, and my breath hisses through the bars of my teeth. My bullet would splatter its head before it had any clue what was happening. I could kill it with a simple squeeze. *Bam.* One less of them in the world.

It takes a lot of effort to ease my finger off the trigger. The sound of the shot will alert others to my presence. There might be hundreds of them, thousands, lurking in the nearby buildings, wandering mindlessly until they catch any sign of prey. They find us by sound, by sight, or by scent. It's too much of a risk to kill this one, and it will gain me nothing.

Keep calm, think logical. Anger only gets you killed.

I watch the thing through my scope as it passes down the empty street, moving between rows of dust-coated cars. It meanders through the trash, the upturned bins, and broken bones. I watch it until it's out of sight. Never take your eyes off them.

"Just animals," I mutter to myself. "They're just animals."

It's not really a comfort. They're not 'just' anything. They're the catastrophe that destroyed the world. They're the deaths of millions.

The sun is well on its way to meet the horizon, and I can't afford to be out at night. During the day, it's a risk, albeit a calculated one. At night, it would be suicide.

At night, the gas will roll back in.

Jack always said it was due to the drop in temperature. He knew more about the gas and its behavior than I did. I just took his word for it and made sure I was always in before dark.

A part of me wants to go out all day and kill as many as I can, like the guy from *I Am Legend*—I forget his name—but I know if I do that, I'll go mad. This isn't about revenge; it can't be. It's about survival. That's why I have to tell myself they're 'just animals' when I know they're much more.

Life is hard, and it doesn't care about revenge. There are no natural laws of justice. There is only survival of the fittest, and if I want to survive, I have to be as hard and cold as life is.

My current base is in a storage center like one of those ones from the auction shows on TV.

It had been Jack's idea and it had proved a good one. The security on the building was solid and there were hundreds of units full of supplies. People stored clothes, blankets, camping equipment. One guy had even stored a bunch of tinned food. He was probably one of those survivalist nuts planning for the apocalypse. The irony hadn't been lost on me as I helped myself.

Still best of all is the security office. It has a heavy door, a comfy chair, and dozens of CCTV screens showing almost every inch of the building and the perimeter. I don't sleep much, but what little rest I do get, I get in that chair, secure in the knowledge that I'll be able to see something coming as soon as I wake.

I bolt the door behind me and sit down, laying my rifle across my lap. A quick glance at my emergency go-bag confirms that it's still in place and untouched, ready for me to grab if I need to make a quick exit. The glances at the bag started as a paranoid twitch but have become a relied-on habit. Too many times, I've been forced to make a panicked escape from a hideout and been left with no supplies, forced to start over again. Go-bags are another thing I learned from Jack.

The bag contains some tinned food, a good knife, a handgun and some ammo, blankets, a compass, a city map, a first aid kit, and a few other odds and ends. It also contains my only photo of Julia, lined with creases and folds and jammed into the first aid kit. Not exactly a great way to honor her memory. It's too painful to look at but I can't throw it away either. That would be like she never existed. I'd thrown away the ultrasound and regretted it every day since.

The rain comes in hard, and there's a rumble of thunder. The storm clouds bring the night in quicker, and the hammering on the metal roof makes me edgy. It's too much like the sound of hundreds of running footsteps. I press the flaps of my hat against my ears—I'm not going to be able to hear danger coming over the rain anyway—and blink the tiredness out of my eyes. I don't want to sleep. Sleep is where memories catch up with you and hold you prisoner.

The rain does a good job of blocking the external cameras, as well as deafening me, but I keep a fevered eye on them regardless, gaze flicking from one to the next in my familiar pattern. For a moment, I think I see something in the corner of the car park near the fence, but there are too many droplets on the lens to tell. It could be just a distortion.

I used to keep an eye out for Jack. He'd almost certainly return here if he could. I'd seen many others come and go, but Jack had always been so calm and certain. He was a hunter and grew up around guns, tracking wild animals with his dad out in Canada. He knew how to survive. If anyone was going to make it out of this hell, it'd be Jack.

"They're just animals," he'd say. "You've got to treat them that way. Dangerous, sure, but just animals. Animals can be avoided. Animals can be killed. They don't strategize. You've just gotta stay smart about it."

It's hard to believe he's gone too.

I feel myself starting to drift so I shift in the chair, shaking my head to try and throw off the heavy drowsiness. I know I can't fight it forever, but I also know that every moment I'm asleep is a moment that I'm vulnerable. It was so much easier when there were two of us. Always one to keep watch.

I loved to watch her sleeping.

It started out as an overprotective thing. As soon as she fell pregnant, I became one of those expectant fathers that freaks whenever his partner stubs their toe or tries to lift so much as a shoebox. It irritated her at first, but she soon fell into teasing me about it. Julia was like that. So easy-going. Always poking fun at me but never hurting my feelings.

I had these nightmares that she'd stop breathing in her sleep, so I started waking up all the time to check on her. My eyes would snap open every half hour or so like clockwork, and I'd listen for her breathing. Then I'd check her anyway to make sure it wasn't my own breath I heard. Until she hit her second trimester and started snoring like a trooper, making that secondary check unnecessary.

After a while, the paranoia about her dying in her sleep faded. I kept checking her because it'd become a habit but also just because I liked to see her looking so peaceful. Even with her mouth wide open and a sound like an angry engine coming out of her nose, she still looked beautiful.

That night though, she was restless. Her face creased with

worry in her sleep. Or was it pain? She moaned and grunted and suddenly sat bolt-upright, clutching her swollen belly.

"What's wrong?" I asked immediately. Since we started coming closer to the due date, I was constantly on alert for the start of her contractions. I had an emergency bag stowed in the car, ready to go. She thought it was ridiculous; she was still weeks away.

"It hurts," she said, her teeth gritted, her back bowed forward over her stomach, both arms wrapped around herself. "It hurts a lot."

"Is it contractions? Do we need to go to the hospital?"

"No, I don't think so—"

The words were barely out of her mouth when she let out a sharp cry and her legs kicked under the blanket.

"Okay, we're going." I leaped from the bed.

Even through the pain, she managed to roll her eyes. "It's not contractions."

"I don't care. If it hurts this much, I'm taking you to the hospital."

I snap awake with a snort, suddenly aware that I've been unconscious. In a panic, my senses bombard me with information that might mean immediate danger. My arms raise the rifle I sleep with automatically, ready to fire. My eyes check the corners of the room (clear), the ceiling (clear), and the door (still bolted). My ears pick up the dull drumming (just the rain on the roof). My nose picks up a musty smell (just my own unwashed clothes).

As my breathing slows, I lower the rifle gently. With the momentary panic over, my thoughts return to the dream.

We'd heard about the gas, of course. They were just vague reports then, on the nightly news. No one was really sure what it was or what it did. The orange-colored fog only appeared at night, in random areas around the country, and it caused massive communication problems in every area it hit. We didn't know back then that this was because there was no one left to communicate with.

Some thought it was a natural phenomenon, some kind of new pollen or even swarms of insects. Others thought it was the result of man-made chemicals interacting with the atmosphere. Of course, the chem-trail crazies thought it was a government conspiracy of one kind or another. Either way, it wasn't a major worry for us. We lived in a nice suburban neighborhood, we didn't think anything could really harm us. It was the same lie everyone tells themselves: it'll never happen to us.

Nobody's safe. That's the real lesson I've learned from all this. Life is cruel and nobody's safe, not even people as mentally strong and well-prepared as Jack.

I glance at the external cameras again. Even now, there's a part of me clinging to the desperate hope that I'll see his hybrid pulling quietly into the car park.

He'd painted it matte black and coated the windows in something to take the shine out of the glass. So long as he kept under a certain speed, the petrol engine didn't kick in and the car was almost silent. We'd used it for night runs a bunch of times. The things were less active at night and the gas masks protected us from the sinister orange cloud. We still tried to avoid it wherever we could, though. There was no sense in chancing fate.

Sometimes we saw it rolling in like a wave of sunset mist, except *that* sounds beautiful and this thing was a foulness, a thick, choking fog that oozed its way over buildings and down streets with an almost palpable malevolence. I couldn't help but personify it, assigning it traits and calling it names. *Evil*, I'd designated it. *Alien. Malicious.* I'd catch myself swearing under my breath when I saw it, not out of fear or awe, but out of sheer hatred.

Jack would caution me when I spoke that way. "All that emotion ain't gonna get you anywhere but dead. And I won't be taken with you. Life's easier with a partner but don't think I won't cut you loose if you can't keep it together. Keep calm, think logical. The fog ain't nothing but fog."

I'd calm myself down grudgingly and settle back into keeping an eye on the distant cloud.

Once parts of the electric grid went down and the city was plunged into darkness, Jack became more eager to do our supply runs at night. He was certain the things had no real night vision.

"It's in their behavior," he'd say. "They don't hunt at night because they're no good at it."

I didn't take much reassurance from that but I'd learned that doing what Jack said kept me alive.

Funny thing about the color orange; if there's no light to shine on it, it just looks black. When we were raiding a local food store in the dark, we didn't see the cloud until it was almost on us.

I freaked when I saw the darkness seep through the door, a rolling wall of pure night.

"Masks," Jack had barked. His orders overrode my panic and talked directly to my muscles, propelling me to grab my mask and slip it on. I also grabbed my gun, as though shooting the gas would do any good. Just holding it made me feel calmer, though. You know things have gone to hell when a thing designed exclusively to kill makes for a good security blanket.

"Steady," Jack warned me as the gas rolled closer.

I heard my own breathing, amplified and weirdly altered by the filter on the mask. I tried to get it under control, but it got faster and faster as the gas came right up to us. It was too late to run now. The logical part of my mind told me that the mask would save me, but I'd seen what the gas could do, and I was terrified.

Then it engulfed us, and I lost sight of everything. I closed my eyes tight but it made no difference; inside the gas cloud, the darkness was total.

"Jack?" I kept my voice low, despite my fear. I didn't want to attract anything that might be listening.

No response.

"Jack?" I called a little louder, straining my ears to hear any sign of him, trying to force my hearing to greater potency.

Still nothing.

He had been standing pretty close when the gas hit but maybe the thickness of the cloud was insulating the sound somehow.

Carefully, I moved, trying to picture the room as it was before it became a pitch-black nightmare. Jack had been only about ten feet away.

I reached out one hand and found the shelf. My arm shook. I couldn't help but think about what would happen if I reached out and touched one of them, something awful and twisted standing so close to me but perfectly hidden.

My feet didn't want to move but I made them. I stayed along the shelves like they were a lifeline, sliding my hand over the wood. Even the noise of my glove on the shelf seemed incredibly loud but I couldn't bring myself to let go.

There was no sign of Jack.

I don't know how long I stood there. Eventually, the gas rolled on like it always does, and the empty air left behind confirmed that I was alone. Had he finally cut me loose after realizing I was no real use to him? Had he simply up and left me in the orange mist? Or had something taken him? Had one of them snatched him without a sound, missing me by pure chance?

I don't think I'll ever know.

The hybrid was still parked outside, but Jack had the keys, so I had to walk back to the storage center. It took hours of careful, tense movements to cross a distance of only a few blocks. I hadn't been so afraid since the night I escaped the museum.

I wake with a start, thunderous gunfire from the museum's corridors still ringing in my ears.

For a moment, I see the dark horror-filled hallways in

front of me as though I'm there, before the dream fades and reality takes hold.

It takes me a heartbeat to realize that the banging hasn't stopped and another to recognize that it isn't gunfire at all but something banging hard on the metal roof.

Frantic, I check the CCTV screens just in time to see one lose signal as the ceiling it was attached to caves in.

I grab my go-bag and my gun but don't head for the exit just yet. I could run straight into them if I don't plan this. Instead, I hover in front of the CCTV screens, like an agitated fly eager to escape a glass bottle. I need to know where they are and how many. If it's just one, I might be able to take it down and continue using this place as my base.

Whatever it is, it's fast.

I can't catch anything on the cameras but a pale blur, thundering its way along the corridors. It seems to be running blind though, which means it doesn't necessarily know I'm in here.

A strange creaking sound makes me turn and what I see makes me raise my gun in panic.

There are fingers slipping beneath the bottom of the security door, curling up to take hold of the wood. Dozens of them, all along the gap, as though a whole group of people are impossibly lying on top of one another in the small corridor beyond. The fingers take a firm grip and begin pulling at the wood.

I'm out of there before it gets through the door, but only just. I hear the wood splintering and a horrible hungry gargling as I slam the roof hatch shut behind me. Jack put this escape route into place not long after we moved in. He never bedded down in a place unless he knew he could get out again in a hurry. I'd never had to use it before.

Keep calm, keep calm. I have to remind myself. It's not easy when you know these things are after you. *Don't run blind. Don't make mistakes.*

I move as quickly as I can across the rain-slick rooftop, glancing over my shoulder constantly for any sign of it. How did it know I was in there? It came straight to the security office once it was inside. *No time to think about that now. Get to the ladder, get to the street.*

The rain pelts me and stings my eyes, making it hard to see. Twice my feet almost slip out from under me as I try to balance my pace between quick and quiet, but I make it to the ladder. It runs down the back wall of the building to the ground.

For a moment, I think there might be more of them waiting for me in the dark below. No streetlights cover the area and I dare not use my torch in case it gives away my position. I don't have a choice now, I realize. There's no other way off the roof and the thing that broke through my door is bound to follow me any minute.

I steel myself and start to climb down the ladder.

I'm not even halfway when the metal groans. I freeze, gripping the cold wet rungs for dear life, but it's too late. There's nothing I can do as the ladder peels away from the wall.

They saw Julia pretty quickly when we got to the hospital.

One nurse fussed around her in the room while the other asked me questions outside the door. Once we were surrounded by medical staff and high-tech equipment, I started to relax. Everything would be okay.

An emergency announcement over the PA system warned us that the gas was coming.

We thought we'd got the window closed in time.

I'm still unsure why whatever wisp of the stuff that got into the room affected only her. Maybe she was in a weakened state, what with the pregnancy. Maybe the air currents just took it that way, and there wasn't enough for everyone. I didn't even realize it was the gas at first; I thought it was something wrong with the baby.

It started with convulsions.

Her back arched, her legs kicked out, and her arms flailed at her sides. Her eyes rolled back in her head. I was screaming for help even though the nurses were already in the room. They shouted medical jargon back and forth and attended to Julia as I stood there helpless.

Two doctors rushed in as her throat started to swell. Within seconds, it was like she'd swallowed a tennis ball whole.

"We're going to need to intubate," shouted one of the doctors. "Airway's obstructed!"

The nurses were holding her down now, her convulsions so violent.

Outside the window, the orange fog looked on.

Even through her swollen throat, her scream was terrible. There was an awful crunch, like a fistful of walnuts snapping and blood sprayed across the ceiling.

A hand reached out from inside her.

At first, I thought it was the baby, even though that was impossible. I watched it grow, the arm rising like a tree in one of those sped-up footage pieces from a nature documentary. A long pale limb, adult and fully formed, reached out of the hole in her chest, a handful of writhing fingers at its end.

The doctors and nurses had stopped working on her. We'd all frozen as more of these limbs tore their way through her torso, reaching towards the ceiling. Her body rose from the bed almost gracefully, her real arms and legs hanging limp as more aberrant limbs emerged through her back, lifting her from the blood-soaked mattress.

The many hands maneuvered themselves, passing her weight between them until they'd twisted her face-down.

Suddenly, her head snapped up to look at one of the doctors. Her expression was twisted into something savage, something hateful. I'd never seen her look like that.

After an inhuman snarl, the limbs propelled her from the bed in a feral pounce, and she bore the woman to the floor, dozens of hands tearing at her, beating her. All the while, the thing that had been Julia yelped and howled.

I was terrified.

The doctor was dead in seconds, beaten to a bloody pulp. Julia leaped at one of the stunned nurses next. I remember noting numbly that some of the doctor's hair was still clumped in several of her new hands.

The nurse's scream woke my body into action. I made no conscious decisions, but my legs propelled me from the room. I slammed the door and pressed my back hard against it, keeping it closed. Shrieks and cries came from elsewhere in the building, but I didn't really register their meaning. I became aware of blood on my face and wiped it away, looking down at red fingertips. I wasn't sure whose it was.

The door thudded at my back, and I whimpered, pressing my weight against it. It banged again, the sound accompanied by a strange gargling whine. She was trying to get out. My wife was a monster, she'd killed everyone in the room, and now she was trying to get out. Trying to get me.

I break the surface of the nightmare-memory with a gasp, lashing out at the past before realizing I'd been dreaming again. My senses filter in almost one at a time as my breathing gradually slows. I hurt all over. I'm lying on something hard and wet. There is rain on my face and blood in my mouth. My head is pounding, and my hand comes away bloody when I touch the back of it. The paltry sunlight, strained through layers of gray cloud, is still enough to hurt my eyes.

I'm not sure what happened until I remember my attempted escape from the storage center and the betrayal of the ladder.

Squinting through the pain, I look up at where the metal had pulled away from the wall. I must have fallen at least twenty feet. How long was I out for?

Panicked, I check my surroundings, each twist of my neck ringing bells of pain up and down my spine. I'd landed in the alley behind the storage center, a thin strip of concrete between the building and the fence, the other side of which was a train yard. Had I really been so lucky as to lie here all night and be overlooked? My watch was broken in the fall so

I have no idea of the time, but it looks to be at least mid-morning.

I can't count on my luck to hold out any longer, though. I need to get out of here as soon as possible and find a new shelter.

As I try to stand, molten agony pours through my left leg and, hissing, I collapse. It takes several minutes for the pain to fade, leaving behind a feeling of deep, cavernous hopelessness. A busted leg could mean the end of me. I try to stand again and find that I can put only the slightest amount of weight on it—anything more is torture. I can't outrun them like this. My only hope is to find shelter and stay put until I'm healed but I don't even know how bad the injury is. Is it just sprained or is this some kind of fracture? Jack would know. I hate him for not being here.

Worse still, my rifle was damaged in the fall, its barrel severely bent. That just leaves me with the handgun in the shoulder holster under my jacket.

Stay calm. Think. Plan. They're just animals and the fog is just fog. They can't strategize—you can. That's how you survive.

I squint up at the clouds, trying to gauge the time of day. My first step to survival is getting somewhere secure as soon as possible.

I use the bent rifle as a walking stick.

With my go-bag slung over my shoulder and my pistol drawn and ready in one hand, I stagger onwards. A part of me just wants to climb inside one of the cargo carriages, pull the doors shut, and wait until night when the creatures are less active. But at night I won't be able to see as well and finding new shelter will be even harder.

The going is painfully slow, literally and figuratively, as I make my way across the train yard. I'm panting hard, which makes it difficult to hear if any of them are nearby and I'm very aware of how much noise my stumbling footsteps make on the gravel.

I haven't been wounded like this since I escaped the hospital, since I found my way—by sheer dumb luck—to the museum.

As a stronghold, it had seemed like a good idea. It was, by nature, a solid structure equipped with great security. It was spacious, heated, and, at least in the wing where we made our home, climate-controlled, which meant the gas couldn't get in.

I wasn't sure how I'd ended up there. After Julia…after she died, I was a broken man.

The people at the museum made me welcome. They were a collection of tattered half-families, grizzled loners, and terrified children, but they had ample supplies and they relied on each other. They gave me food and an area to sleep in. They treated my wounds and gave me company. They also gave me a sense of security, something I never thought I'd feel again. I still woke up crying out in fear each night but at least, once I was awake, I knew I was safe.

It was at the museum that I heard the most varied theories about the gas.

One woman, Caroline, had been a lab tech at a water treatment plant and was a keen scientist. She'd read an article about a radical new treatment in development for amputees that proposed the use of stem cells to regrow entire limbs. Caroline was convinced the gas was related to that.

Another of the survivors there, Paul, was certain the gas somehow reactivated what he called 'recombinant DNA,' which he explained as being all the junk in our genes from the various stages of our evolution that just isn't active anymore.

Of course, some people thought aliens were to blame, or that it was some kind of terrorist attack, but none of them were as impassioned as Caroline. She was almost manic about it. One of the other women, Janine, told me that Caroline had lost two kids to the gas and they'd killed her husband once they turned.

Perhaps that's why we found her one night, smothering the children in their sleep.

The resultant gunfire broke one of the sturdy windows and the gas, pressed against the glass like some perverted watcher, was free to billow in.

The rest of that night had been a nightmare of chaos and panic as we fled from the orange fog. I remember catching a glimpse of Paul, screaming as the gas overwhelmed him. He staggered forward, trying to reach for help as a series of sickening crunches sounded from inside him, each one signaling the change of his joints to a new, inhuman position. A violent convulsion threw him to the ground as his legs bent to new shapes. His face turned to me, the skin writhing like a stormy ocean, blood pooling from his mouth as his teeth fell out.

I shake myself out of the memory. I'm not sure if it's the tiredness, the events of last night, or the blood loss that's making it hard to focus on the present but if I don't stay sharp, I'll end up dead.

I come back to reality just in time to hear one of them close by, crunching across the gravel. As I freeze, crouched against one of the dormant rusting carriages, it stalks into view.

It moves on four legs, the knees of the rear two inverted. Its fore-limbs are more like arms and it carries its weight on worn, flat knuckles in a gorilla-like gait. Where the head would be on any normal quadruped, there is instead another spinal column, curving upwards from the shoulders like a grotesque centaur. This second torso is all but a skeleton, thinly held together by bright red ropes of tendon and muscle. The grisly skull at the summit of the monster is only partially formed and, through the gaps in its cranium, I see something fleshy, beating like a heart.

It turns towards me before I can hide, and I thank god that it has no eyes. Instead, it seems to be seeking me out by hearing, tilting its grizzly head to one side. I try not to breathe but it seems to hear me anyway, shuffling slowly closer on two feet and a hand while the other crawls its way across the metal wall of the train car.

If I stay here, it will find me. If I move, it might hear me. No choice.

Moving as slowly and carefully as I can, my heart hammering so loud I'm sure the creature will hear it, I lower myself to the ground. I don't want to take my eyes off it, but I have no choice as I'm forced to turn my head to fit under the carriage. I can smell the stink of the creature, old blood and stale piss, looming over me as I painstakingly slide under the metal frame, desperate not to make a noise on the gravel. I won't know it's found me until it drags me out.

The sky is much darker by the time I painfully crawl from my hiding place. I'm not sure if it's later than I thought or if the clouds are gathering. Either way, it's not a good sign. I have to make it out of the train yard and across the highway before I reach even the closest buildings. There's no guarantee any of them will be suitable. Or empty.

By the time I leave the train yard, it's clear I'm not going to make it inside before dark.

The streetlights over the highway have come on—this part of the city evidently still has power—which means dusk can't be far away. I'm exhausted. I need to get somewhere, anywhere, where I can rest. I don't know when I last ate, I don't know how much blood I've lost, but I know for sure that limping along like this is sapping what little energy I have.

Even if I could make it to the buildings, it's a painstaking process making sure they're clear and finding a defensible room.

I start to get angry. If it hadn't been for that stupid ladder, if I had prepared the escape route better, if I hadn't fallen. I grit my teeth against the parade of torturous ifs circling in my mind. They won't help me now. I need to get out of the open, by any means necessary.

That's when I hear something that makes my blood freeze.

A horrible pattering. Hundreds of hands smacking against the floor.

In an instant, I'm taken back to the dark corridors of the hospital, the night Julia died.

The power had gone out only a few minutes after the gas rolled in. I'm sure hospitals are supposed to have backup generators and things like that, but they didn't kick in and I was left in near-total darkness with the screaming.

I'd managed to get away from Julia by shoving a stretcher in front of the door to her room and running as fast as I could. I'd fled blind through the corridors, trying to find my way out but the place was a maze.

Julia wasn't the only one who'd been changed by the fog.

The hospital was a nightmare of gibbering monstrosities. Blood drenched the walls. Bodies, beaten and mutilated, were scattered everywhere. I tried not to look at them. Some had tooth marks in their flesh. Others were in pieces.

Something awful was happening in pediatrics. I made the mistake of glancing through the glass panel in the door. Most of the corridor was taken up by a large mass, a dark slope with a human torso at its peak, its bald head just a few inches below the tiles of the ceiling.

A flash of light from outside, maybe from a passing car, gave me a glimpse of the abomination.

The lower slopes of the thing writhed, glistening. Hundreds of worms coiled and tangled, slowly slithering over and around each other. Not worms, I realized in a moment of appalling understanding, but guts. The intestines of the thing had spilled and multiplied and now they spread like questing roots from a macabre tree, slick with blood and mucus.

I watched, cemented in place by horror, as the thing dragged the unconscious body of an orderly, loops of serpentine digestive tract wrapped around his legs. As he disappeared into the mass, the thing let out a long, low, damp moan, shuddering with pleasure.

When I heard the *pitter-patter* of dozens of agile hands, I knew she'd come for me. There must have been hundreds of people in the hospital when the gas rolled over it and at least a dozen of those must have been changed by it. The chances of her tracking me down, singling me out of a crowd that size, should have been tiny. I knew she'd find me anyway. I knew it was me she wanted.

I turned from the glass and saw her charging, spider-like, down the corridor towards me.

I hobble as fast as I can onto a bus and fold the doors shut.

Dragging myself into the aisle, I duck below the seats and hold my breath, praying that whatever it is doesn't see me. I know it's close; the rapid *pat-pat-pat* of its feet was loud.

I hold my pistol close, cradling it against my chest. Small caliber rounds aren't great against a lot of them, especially if they've got weird bone growths or their vital organs are in weird places. I have to pray it'll be enough.

I feel like breaking down in tears. The running, the hiding, the constant fear and tension, I just can't take it anymore. This isn't how it was supposed to be. I'm supposed to be with Julia, painting a bedroom blue or pink and getting into arguments at 3 a.m. about whose turn it is to comfort the crying baby. Instead, I'm in a constant nightmare where every single thing is twisted and cruel. There's no comfort. There's no hope.

The thing slams itself against the window of the bus and I jump.

Four hands with long fingers press against the glass, a pair on either side of an emaciated face. Its eyes have melted away, their jelly staining the withered, hollow cheeks below. I can't be sure what age it was before the fog changed it, but there's a child-like quality to its features, like a nightmarish cherub. It opens its mouth slowly and impossibly wide, its jaw unhinging to dangle in front of its throat. From between two rows of healthy-looking human teeth, a tongue the size of my hand emerges. It hits the glass with a muffled wet thud. At the center of this pock-marked muscle, a single eye flicks open. The tiny pupil fixes on me, practically vibrating with hatred.

The tongue retracts, the jaw crunches back into place and the creature begins beating its fists against the windows, screaming bloody murder.

Suddenly, I'm filled with the will to live again. It's probably a purely biological reaction to danger. Fight or flight or whatever. Raw chemistry demanding I survive this.

I raise my gun to the monster. As soon as it breaks through, I'll shoot it in the head and get the hell away from here. There's no guarantee a headshot will work on this thing; there may not even be a brain inside that skull, but I'll cross that bridge when I come to it.

It's then that I realize the thing outside the window isn't my biggest problem.

It's the gas.

The gas is pouring between the buildings like a tidal wave. I'm trapped.

Panicking, I forget my gun and fumble in my go-bag for the mask. My frantic heartbeat drowns out the pounding on the windows. I pull the gas mask free from the go-bag's other contents and the bottom drops out of my stomach.

The filter is broken. Part of it falls away as I lift the mask up. I must have damaged it when I fell from the rooftop.

I look back to the windows, now webbed with cracks from the beating they've taken. Any second now, the creature will smash them and the gas will pour in. There's nothing I can do.

The gas spreads around the bus slowly, like an octopus around a bottle with a fish trapped inside. I can sense its smug satisfaction. It's waited all this time for me. It knew I'd never escape.

The glass shatters and the gas oozes its way in, crawling over the seats towards me. I shuffle backwards as far as I can, frantic to keep out of its reach but I know it's no good. All I can do is take one last breath of non-lethal air and hold it as long as possible.

I can't see or hear the creature anymore. The unwelcome embrace of the orange fog has become my whole world. My lungs burn as I try to keep it from entering me—another hopeless act of defiance—but I can't hold my breath forever.

The first deep gasp brings searing pain almost instantly.

My throat slams shut like a trap, preventing me from screaming but the gas is already inside. My bones feel like they're melting. My skin bubbles as I start to fit, limbs in spasm.

In my last moments, I think of Julia.

I think of the smell of her hair and how it came out in bloody clumps.

I think of the feel of her skin, her fingers around my throat, choking the life out of me.

I think of her big brown eyes. I remember how one of them was knocked from its socket as I caved in her skull with a fire extinguisher.

I have nothing left. Not my memories. Not my own body.

As the pain reaches a point beyond anything I've ever known, I feel a hand pushing at my chest.

Pushing from the inside.

DISPERSION

Three days into treatment, my lungs shut down.

I'd gone to the hospital because I was having trouble breathing. My chest felt tight and dried out. A cough had torn my throat ragged over a few days and it refused to budge despite all the store-bought medication I glugged down. I'd expected to be prescribed some antibiotics and sent on my way, embarrassed to have wasted their time but relieved it was nothing more serious. Instead, after some basic prodding and tests, I was immediately isolated in my own room.

The doctors would only answer my questions with questions of their own. Had I been overseas in the last 9 months? Did I come into contact with any exotic flora or fauna? Where did I buy my groceries? I demanded to know what was going on, but I was met with words like *precautionary measures* and *just protocol* from behind their masks. They came and went a dozen times in a dozen hours for more blood and more samples and more questions.

"Who have you been in contact with recently?"

"I've told you already: no one! I live alone. I work from home. I don't even have pets! Tell me what's going on right now or I swear to god, I will get up and walk right out of here!"

It was an idle threat, I knew; the door of my room only opened via some kind of security pass. I was angry and tired and *still* coughing, so reason wasn't at the forefront of my mind. The doctor was caught by his own pity. I saw the struggle in his eyes before he relented and pulled up a stool to sit by my bedside.

"There is a fungal infection in your lungs." His tone was somber and his eyes stayed on mine. "At least, it's in your lungs for now. At the rate it's spreading…well, we're not sure where it will go after that."

"How do we get rid of it? When can I go home?"

"We're still looking for answers. We're not even sure what it is beyond some kind of fungus. We've never seen anything like it and it's proven resilient to all standard treatments."

The sudden dryness in my mouth had nothing to do with my condition. "What are you saying?"

"We're doing everything we can. We're running every test possible. Specialists are flying in from all over. We have to be very careful that it doesn't spread since we have no idea what its capabilities are. That's why you're alone in here."

The second day was hell.

I rolled around in thick, gray sweat, unable to comprehend primate voices. Sound distorted like a broken mirror. I heard myself mumbling but even I didn't know what I was saying.

They strapped my arms down to stop me from thrashing.

They dimmed the lights when my skin started to burn.

Resurfacing to consciousness, I found them crowded around my bed. My vision swam but I forced focus. The doctors looked at each other, at their machines, at their charts. They were confused. The sounds they made were untranslatable, alien broadcasts on the air.

The last words I'd understood echoed in my mind:

Alone in here. Alone in here. Alone in here.

It hurt less now. My throat was raw from coughing but, in the dark, my skin no longer burned.

My body had ballooned, my arms swollen almost to the point of enveloping the straps. I couldn't see my legs over my belly. I tried to move, groaning with the effort of lifting my head. One of the doctors reached over. To undo the straps? To comfort me? The slick grayness on my skin burned through the acrid latex glove and he was taken screaming from the room.

His blood tasted sweet on my arm.

My chest wasn't moving. A lifetime of respiratory rhythm had ceased. Unencumbered by the heavy flesh of lungs, I had never breathed so clearly. I drank the air in through my skin and knew relief.

I grew in the warm and the dark. *Alone, alone, alone.* My eyes were swallowed up in the folds of my face but I didn't need them anymore. My jaw broke under the pressure of flesh but there was no pain. I knew heat, I knew moisture, and I knew light. These were my senses now and nothing else seemed important. Time became a metric I no longer understood. Only expansion was measurable and I flooded into every available space.

Living things were heat to me. I felt the warmth of their alien forms in the air and couldn't remember what they were called. Somewhere I knew that I used to be like them, but that existence was a strange and distant dream now.

I found cold, sterile borders and my expansion was forced to halt. The other living things ceased to register and I understood that they had sealed me inside. They sought to destroy me, to starve me to death.

I tested the walls of this prison, taking root in every corner, pressing into every crack to find a way out. There was none. I was trapped. I would die of thirst here.

I retreated into myself. My body had dried up, shriveled, and died. I was a small thing again, inside this husk of flesh; not so small as I had once been, but greatly reduced.

Their presence woke me as they entered my space. I could taste the moisture inside them. I didn't understand them at all any longer, these singular creatures. Each body was only one thing, adrift in a void, not connected to any other. They were alone. I teemed with life.

I *was* life.

I let go of my form. My body collapsed. Dried out and useless, it was too broken to be revived. I freed myself into the air, a million tiny fragments of self, each one whole and apart at once. Carried on the currents, I was free at last. I would grow again in a thousand different spaces, all connected. I would expand.

No longer alone.

INTO THE WALLS

Sadie didn't like the smell of the new house. It smelled like plastic and bleach. The water tasted like chemicals and the light at night was too bright. Great orange slabs of it came through her curtains and she couldn't see the stars.

This house had all the wrong noises too. There were no owls, no distant moo-cows or farm dogs barking. No wood creaking and settling, only plastic floors that made her feet feel sticky and the weird buzzing of the fridge. Outside was a constant grumbling of cars and smoke and strange alarms. The winding traffic below her window was like a great multicolored snake, slithering over black rocks, on its way to nowhere. The snake had no head and no tail, and it went on forever.

"Why did we come here, Mummy?" Sadie had asked many times, always hoping for a different answer. If she got a new answer, maybe she would be able to convince Mummy of just how bad an idea it all was.

"Because of Mummy's job," was what she was always told. Sadie had run out of ways to try and argue with that. She knew the job was important to Mummy. She didn't want to be what Aunty Beth called 'a difficult child.' Still, she knew this place was all wrong.

Rocco didn't like it either but he was only a gerbil so Mummy and Daddy didn't listen to him. He burrowed himself in bedding outside his little wooden hut and wouldn't come out. Sadie understood what he meant: home wasn't home anymore.

Mummy's job started straight away, so she was gone every day before Sadie woke up. Daddy spent most of his day in the office room. Micah's crib was in there so that Daddy could keep an eye on him.

School hadn't begun yet, so Sadie was left to entertain herself all day. Micah was too young to play with, but he seemed to enjoy her funny faces, so she leaned over the crib, pushed out her cheeks, and blew raspberries at him.

"Sweetie, please!" Daddy didn't turn around, but she knew his face was all stressed. "Daddy needs to work. Can you play somewhere else?"

Daddy frowned a lot these days and he was always muttering under his breath. Sadie sometimes heard bad words in those mutters, but she didn't dare say anything about it. Daddy never used to say those things.

"Okay." Sadie quietly slid from the room and Daddy's tapping at the computer resumed.

With nowhere to go, she drifted around the apartment, like dust carried on the air conditioning.

They had brought lots of things from home: Daddy's favorite chair, all of Mummy's books, and Sadie's toys and games, but the place still felt empty. The ceilings had no wooden beams and were much higher up. They looked like a cold, gray sky and Sadie felt that grayness in her heart. Always, she felt the presence of space.

Sadie avoided the kitchen. At the old house, the kitchen had been a warm place with delicious smells and big wooden chairs. This kitchen was all squeaky plastic and hard metal and had tall uncomfortable stools to sit on. It was cold and Sadie felt unwelcome there.

She ended up in the same spot as always: the little chair by the living room window. From there, she could see into the other apartments, where the building curved in on itself in a U-shape. She knew it was rude to look into other people's houses, but she wasn't doing it to be rude, so it was probably okay.

She stared at the old lady's window. She found it easily because of the window boxes full of flowers. The old lady watered and trimmed them so delicately that Sadie thought she must be a lovely, gentle person. Sometimes there was a young man with her, and Sadie imagined it was her son visiting and that the old lady made him cookies and told him stories.

Two windows down and two across from her were a young couple. Sadie had named them Jack and Lily in her head. Lily had a cup of coffee each morning while looking out of her window, but she didn't see Sadie watching. Jack always seemed busy in the kitchen. Sadie imagined he was a famous chef and was always coming up with new meals.

On the next row down and all the way in the corner, right at the edge of Sadie's sight, was the boy's room. Sadie couldn't tell much about him because it was difficult to see, but he was about her age, she thought.

A lot of the apartments were empty. Mummy said this was because the building was new and was still filling up with people, but Sadie thought that it was because the building was all wrong and people didn't like it there. The building didn't seem new to her. It was shiny and it was clean but there was a big feeling of age in it, like an old dark tree with deep roots. Sadie had already seen the lights go off in one apartment and they never came back on. She was sure the people there were gone.

Nights were the worst in the new house.

Sadie lay in the dark, unable to sleep beneath the too-big ceiling. The space made her feel like a baby bunny caught under an open sky where hungry hawks might be circling. It stretched, even as Sadie watched, and she knew it was making a space for her to fall up into. She'd never get back out. She gripped the bed tight, terrified to fall asleep and let go, but there was only so long she could stay awake for.

In her nightmares, the room stretched so much that the

walls cracked, and her blankets and toys were sucked inside. She ran to find Mummy and Daddy, but they had already gone into the walls and she was left alone in the hungry rooms.

The nightmares got so bad that she would wake and cry out until Daddy came to her room, but he didn't comfort her like he used to. Instead, he told her off for being noisy.

"Mummy and Daddy have to work in the morning." His teeth were too tight when he spoke, and his eyes were angry. "You're too old for this nonsense."

Sadie didn't cry out after that, but the nightmares just got worse, especially after Rocco escaped. At first, she thought he was hidden somewhere in his bedding, but he wasn't anywhere in the cage. Daddy said that he must have gotten out, but Sadie didn't see how.

He was just gone.

There was a crack in the living room wall, hair-thin and only as long as her finger, but Sadie was sure it hadn't been there before. She stared at it for a long time before poking it with a pencil just to be sure. The pencil didn't get sucked in. Maybe it was just a normal crack. Maybe it had been there all along.

She went to the office to tell Daddy, even though she knew he was cross all the time now. Mummy was home less and less, and Daddy was more and more angry. They barely spoke to her and they wouldn't listen. Sadie wasn't sure if it had been days or weeks but she knew it was all just getting worse.

When she crept into the office, plucking up the courage to talk to Daddy, she realized that Micah's crib was empty.

"Daddy, where's Micah?"

"Not now, Sadie. Can't you see I'm busy?"

"But Micah's not here, Daddy." Had Mummy taken him to work? No, that didn't make sense. Mummy's work was much too busy to have a baby there.

"Who? Look, just go and play somewhere else."

"But—"

"Get out, Sadie!" Daddy stood up and shouted so suddenly that Sadie almost fell over. As she scrambled out of the room, he strode after her and slammed the door.

Just for a moment, before she was shut out, she thought she saw cracks in his face.

Sadie knew she shouldn't leave the apartment, but she also knew she had to. Micah was missing and there was something wrong with Daddy. She didn't know how to call Mummy and there was no one else except the people she'd seen from her window. The nice old lady or Jack and Lily would help her. Someone had to help her.

Sadie put on her shoes, took a deep breath, and quietly slipped through the front door and out into the building.

It was bright and wide and cold in the corridors. Sadie leaned against the wall, feeling wobbly. One footstep at a time and taking deep breaths, she made her way towards the stairs. From there, she would work out how to get to those other apartments.

She remembered the way to the stairs from Move-In Day. It had been an adventure then, playing in boxes and dreaming up what the new house would look like. They'd been happy, the three of them.

"Four," she said out loud. "Micah was there too."

She frowned. How could she have forgotten about Micah? And where were the stairs? She should have found them by now; they were only two turns from the front door. Instead, there were only more walls and more doors. Everything was so cold, and it all looked the same. Sadie felt a shiver across her skin and in her heart, but she knew she had to keep going, for her brother's sake.

Sadie felt like she'd been walking for hours. The corridors wound around and around but never went anywhere. Her footsteps echoed loudly, and she could see her own breath. She still hadn't found the stairs or a way around to the rest of the building, so far as she could tell. There were no windows, so she couldn't check.

She listened at the doors but didn't dare to knock. All was quiet and she knew that meant that anything lurking would hear her knocking. There was nowhere to hide in the corridors and nothing to hold onto if a crack opened up to swallow her. She didn't hear anything behind any of the doors either. The whole building felt empty.

Just as she was ready to give up, Sadie heard a movement. Someone else's footsteps were coming along behind her. Fear gripped her tight. She wanted to run but her legs wouldn't move. Her mind imagined a hundred horrors that might come around the corner at any moment.

A small pale face beneath a dark fringe peered around at her. They locked eyes for several moments in silence.

"You're the boy from the window," Sadie said, her fear easing a little.

"You're real." The boy eased around the corner a little. He was terribly pale, and he held himself in as small a shape as possible, shoulders all hunched in.

"Real? Of course, I'm real."

"Not everyone here is real."

"What do you mean by that?"

"The ones who go into the walls, they don't come back real. They come back something else."

Sadie tried to ignore the chill his words gave her. "I need your help. Something's wrong with this place. The baby...I mean, my brother is missing. Where are your parents?"

"They went into the walls a long time ago. They're not even Not Real anymore. They're just gone."

Sadie backed away. The boy was staring at her and it made her uneasy.

"I don't know what you mean," she said. "Can you please just help me? I need to find the baby."

"I can't help you. No one can. It's the emptiness of this place, I think. It wants to be filled so it fills itself up with people."

Sadie backed off further. She didn't like the boy. His voice was flat and dead, and his eyes were dark. "I think I should go home," she said, though she didn't want to turn her back on him.

"I wish I could. I don't think I have a home anymore."

With that, he slid back around the corner, keeping his eyes on her until the last possible moment. Then he was gone.

Sadie had worried about finding her way home through the maze of corridors, but it was easy. She wasn't sure if it was just chance that she was close or if something strange was going on. She slipped into the apartment as quietly as possible so as to not disturb Daddy. The office door was still closed.

Mummy wasn't home yet and Sadie didn't know what else to do. Feeling miserable and alone, she went back to the seat by the window and looked out.

She found the old lady's window first, but all of her flowers were dead and black in their boxes. How long had it been since they'd been watered? It couldn't have been that long, could it? The old lady was nowhere to be seen.

Lily drank her coffee alone, staring into nothing. Jack wasn't in the kitchen. The lights were off in there.

The boy wasn't at his window. She wondered if he was still drifting like a ghost through the corridors.

Feeling more alone than ever, Sadie went to her room. On her way, she checked the crack in the wall. It was longer than before by a finger length.

She tried not to sleep but sleep came anyway and brought more nightmares with it. She ran down endless corridors. The walls cracked and crumbled behind her. Each new dark split dragged at her hair and clothes like a storm wind. She knew it was the breath of the building, that it was trying to suck her up like spaghetti.

When that didn't work, the things came out to get her.

Pale hands first, gripping the edges of the cracks and pulling themselves free. They were shaped like people but all wrong, all flat and cold and faded, pale and stretched like they were drawn on white paper from memory. They staggered after her, more and more of them, and when they caught her, they dragged her screaming into the dark.

She woke up to a terrible tearing noise, like a huge sheet of paper ripping. Her room was dark, and her door was still shut. She was sure the noise came from the living room and she was sure she knew what it was.

She crept to the bedroom door and opened it carefully.

The living room had become vast, stretched out so big that she couldn't see the ceiling in the darkness. The crack was tearing its way up the wall, leaving no dust or debris, ripping deeper and taller with every second. Inside it was pure black. The stomach of the building.

The woman's coat was on the hook, but Sadie knew she wasn't home. She struggled to picture the woman but, no matter how hard she tried, she could only get fragments. The smell of her hair. How her laugh sounded.

Daddy's office door was closed. He had to listen now. If she could just show him the crack, he couldn't be angry. He'd see she was right all along.

The crack was between her and the door. She would have to walk past it to reach Daddy.

Dare she call out to him? Even if he came to shout at her, he would still see the crack. But what if something in the crack heard her? She remembered what the boy said about things coming out of the walls. She remembered the twisted people from her nightmares. She couldn't stand to make a sound that might draw them out.

Sadie crept forward, keeping her eyes on the crack. Each step took forever. Her toes stung against the cold floor and her fearful tears froze on her cheeks. Was something moving in the crack or was it her imagination? Was the apartment getting bigger again? She couldn't tell. It took all her willpower to keep her feet shuffling forward.

She was nearly at the door. The tearing sound came again but her heart was pounding so loud, she could barely hear it. The crack grew larger still.

Her hand shaking, she reached out for the handle, turned it, and stepped inside.

The office was empty.

Something moved behind her.

A white hand came out of the darkness of the crack, gripping the edge from the inside, just like she'd dreamed. Sadie was frozen to the spot as the monster pulled itself free from the darkness. It was tall, with long arms and legs and too-long fingers. It was white, its clothes, its hair. It cast no shadow.

It was Daddy.

Where his face should have been was one big crack into darkness.

Sadie screamed and slammed the office door.

Daddy tried to get into the office for a long time, but he never turned the handle. Maybe he couldn't remember how. Sadie curled up in the corner and hugged her knees until the banging stopped. She stayed there even longer in silence. She didn't know if he was still out there or if he'd gone back into the walls. She didn't know which was worse.

There was a crib in the room, but Sadie couldn't remember who it was for. She wanted to go home but she couldn't remember where that was. She couldn't remember anywhere but the apartment. A window let cold, gray light into the room. Outside, the building went on forever, curving in on itself again and again. The building was the sky. The building was the ground. There was no escape and nowhere to escape to. She was trapped.

She saw the dead flowers in their window boxes. There was something moving in the old lady's apartment, something thin and pale. She was gone.

She saw Jack strangle Lily. His face was all cracked. When she stopped struggling, he dragged her into the walls.

There were no other lights left on. There was no one left to help Sadie. There was no one left at all.

Sadie went back into the living room. The man who had banged on the door was gone but the crack was still there, yawning bigger than ever, a mouth that had eaten everything she'd ever known.

As she stepped towards it, pale hands reached out to drag her into the dark.

EXIT PROGRAM Y/N?

My fingers screeched to a halt over the Y button, defying years of administrative muscle memory. This particular piece of software had a habit of crashing if you closed it this way. The resultant catastrophic failure would delete all data entered that day, even if it had been previously saved.

We had been told by our increasingly frustrated manager that I.T. was working on a fix. The sweat on his brow whenever the topic of the new systems was raised—which was done frequently and at volume—told us the truth. No matter what words he used, what he really meant was, *"Look, the company spent a lot of money on this software and we're all stuck with it, like it or not."*

I gritted my teeth, navigating the various menus to close the program without eradicating my morning's work. I'd fallen into that pitfall several times already this week. I would've preferred to leave the damn thing running until the end of the day but another delightful foible of this recent 'upgrade' was that it seemed to overheat any computer that attempted to run it for more than an hour.

"Shut down again? I can hear your teeth grinding from here."

I couldn't actually see Mark behind his dual monitor set-up but I could hear the exasperation in his tone. He sounded like I felt.

"Hrrn," was my noise of confirmation. "Might want to

close yours too. I can hear the fan spinning up. Sounds like a jet engine getting ready for take-off."

"Like a washing machine full of bricks, more like. My PC was fucked long before they installed this crap on it." He leaned back in his chair, bringing himself into my field of view while he pinched his nose, glasses removed and held in his other hand. "All that money and it's not even sleek to look at. I hate every Windows update but at least they generally look clean."

"It's hideous," Jess chimed in over the top of the divider between our desks. "Who puts light-blue font on a lilac background? I feel like it's going to make my eyes bleed."

Mark got done pinching his nose and rubbing his eyes and shot me a look. "Lunch?"

I checked the clock. "Five minutes early but, yeah, sod it. They owe us the time for putting us through this hell."

Standing and stretching brought the rest of the office into view. Fifteen desks, crammed together beneath dirty yellow electric lights. Each one housed a frustrated human clicking away at little boxes on their screens in a vain attempt to get some work done between system crashes. Paul had his face so close to his monitor that his nose almost touched it. Karen was on the phone and, judging by the mess of scrambled lilac graphics on her display, I could guess who she was calling. She rolled her eyes at me and I shrugged my powerless sympathies before following Mark out of the room.

It was raining so we stayed in the drab little cafeteria on the third floor.

The lighting there was no less grubby and the hum of the bulbs was pervasive but at least large windows afforded us a view of the outside world, such as it was. A large billboard overlooked the main road, advertising the latest Xbox.

Mark munched his sandwich and massaged his eyes some more, glasses discarded on the plastic table between us. I chomped moodily on my crisps. The vending machine was out of salt and vinegar again, so I was stuck with cheese and onion.

"The whole thing stinks of one of those management decisions. The ones where something gets implemented without checking with the ground-level people who are actually going to be affected."

I grunted in agreement. It was unfortunate but not surprising. A lot of management decisions seemed to go that way. Just like when they took away the coffee machine.

"It's just like when they took away the coffee machine." Mark read my mind. His mouthful of sandwich was no barrier to expressing his outrage. "They couldn't be arsed to pay to fix it so they took it away without even thinking about us. It's always about the bottom line and not the people working on it."

I didn't need to reply. My agreement on the subject was an unspoken certainty.

"I feel like my eyes have grit in them." He rubbed them again. They were bloodshot now, but how much of that was down to screen fatigue and how much to his incessant prodding was anyone's guess.

I looked around the cafeteria for a change of subject. It was bad enough working with the problem software, I didn't want to talk about it all the time too. "Pretty empty in here."

"Yeah, there's a bug going around, I heard. Headaches, vomiting, all that stuff. So at least there's that to look forward to. At least it would get me away from those damn screens for a bit. I've never even heard of Raylleigh Software Solutions, or however you pronounce it. What is that? Finnish or something?"

I shrugged, giving up on trying to steer us from this path. Mark wasn't done venting, it seemed. I tuned out and stared through the window. As my gaze landed on the billboard, a bird collided with it and struck itself dead, body spiraling onto the street below. All that sky and it managed to hit something so comparatively small. I shook my head at the stupidity of birds.

"Damn printer's gone berserk." John ran a stressed-out hand through his increasingly wild hair and frowned at the pages spewing from the mouth of the machine.

"What's wrong with it?"

"Keeps printing this gobbledygook instead of my charts."

He held up a handful of papers. Line after line of some weird symbols, the kind that every word processor seems to come with but I never understood why.

"I've got a meeting in an hour. What am I going to do for handouts?"

"Put it on a USB and use a projector," Mark suggested. "Save the environment. And put a call into I.T. about the printer. I'm holding out hope that if we keep reporting the problem, they'll have to do something."

"Fat chance," grunted John. He abandoned the printer to its strange emissions and picked up his phone. "Honestly, all this progress as a species and we still can't work out wire-less-bloody-printing."

"Maybe the I.T. guys will appreciate a printer problem in the sea of software issues," I suggested.

"Ha! As if they're not related."

"Jesus!" John flinched away from the handset. "Some kind of weird feedback noise. Like screeching."

"Oh, great. So phone systems are down too? Bloody typical."

I unlocked the computer, determined to ignore Mark's unstoppable torrent of negativity. I still had targets to hit by the end of the day.

The error message flashed at me for the hundredth time and I frowned back at it.

A constant hum of electrical equipment made my brain feel numb and I became aware of grit in my eyes. *Time for a screen-break.* "Anyone else got this date error?" I asked. "I keep putting it in but it bounces back as incorrect."

"You've got to use today's date," said Jess's voice over the divider.

"Yeah, thanks. I am." It came out harsher than I meant it and I immediately felt guilty. In penance, I double-checked the date on my watch. "Can't be right," I muttered to myself, holding the watch to my ear to listen for the tick of life in the device. "My watch says 24th."

"Well, congratulations, you've got a watch that works." A grouchy reply from Jess but I deserved it.

I stared back at the box on the screen where I'd been typing 15th over and over and getting nowhere. "I guess I had a brain-fart or something."

Karen started to hum a little tune, something she'd picked up after hours on the phone to I.T. I scowled in her direction as though all my woes were her fault.

Mark leaned back in his chair to catch my attention. "Lunch?" His eyes were red raw.

"Yeah, I could use a break. Must be losing my marbles."

The cafeteria was deserted.

I stared out the window while Mark munched his sandwich. When did I last eat? I couldn't remember. I couldn't remember going home, feeding the cat, sleeping. What had I done with the last nine days?

"I think I need a holiday," I said.

"We all do."

Across the street I watched a bird plough into the billboard, falling onto the pile below.

Darryl vomited into his bin as we returned to the office.

"Jesus, Darryl! If you're ill, go home, mate."

"I'malrgihh." He wiped his face and returned his attention to the screen.

"It reeks! Someone get rid of it."

Instinctively, I grabbed the little waste bin and rushed it hastily to the bathroom before the smell could gain a foothold in the office. The vomit was viscous and a rusty brown color. Unsure what else to do, I tipped the contents into the toilet and left the bin for the cleaners. Just before I hit the flush, I was sure something moved down in that brown muck.

Something slender and eel-like.

There was nothing there when the water cleared.

John slammed his handset down as I came back in. "Bloody feedback noise. Sounds like an old dial-up modem being tortured to death."

"So even I.T. has abandoned us," Mark grumbled.

"We could just go to their floor and see them?" I suggested.

Silence followed this suggestion.

"Don't all jump up at once! I'll bloody go. What's the problem, John?"

"Hmm?" John had gone back to staring at his screen.

"The problem. I.T. Hello?"

"Oh, everything. Bloody printer."

"Alright. The printer. Jesus, it's like pulling teeth." I frowned at John, the lilac light of the monitor filling his eyes.

With his free hand, he absentmindedly doodled on a scrap of paper, copying the symbols the printer had been producing.

I.T. was only two floors up so I took the stairs. That was my policy: any more than two and I felt entitled to the laziness of the lift.

I regretted that decision before long. My legs burned and I was out of breath by the time I'd got to the next landing. I frowned at my own body. Surely I wasn't that out of shape? I hadn't been great with the gym recently but one flight of stairs shouldn't be enough to do me in. I caught my breath and wiped the sweat off my brow.

By the fifth flight, I was wheezing. This wasn't right. There should've been a door by now, an exit to the next floor. I leaned over the railing and squinted up and down the stairwell but no answers made themselves known. Was I losing it?

The lights went out.

There were no windows in the stairwell; it was a hollow concrete cuboid that echoed every footstep. With the lights off, I couldn't see my hand in front of my face.

Thankfully, the safety lights kicked in a moment later and bathed the stairs in soft lilac light. Puffing out relief that I wouldn't have to fumble my way out in the dark, I continued the climb.

I was so overjoyed to see the door that I flung myself against it, half expecting it to disappear like a desert mirage. Instead, I stumbled into the corridor beyond.

The lights were out here, too, but I could still read the sign on the wall: a big blue five. I'd definitely gone up more flights than that. Between that and the missing days, I was starting to think I needed a holiday sooner rather than later.

Drenched in sweat and seeking refreshment, I headed straight for the water cooler, which I could barely make out in the lilac gloom. I inhaled deeply between gulps of water as the cooler burbled away. When something thumped against the inside, I almost choked.

I yanked my hand back from where I'd been leaning on the bottle and squinted into its contents. It should've been easy to see inside the clear container but something about the lilac light and the smoky shadows it produced rendered the water strangely opaque. I was sure I saw something move.

Something long and eel-like.

Disgusted, I discarded the rest of the cup and tried to calm myself. This was some kind of breakdown. Workplace stress. That kind of thing. I was losing it. Things did not live in water coolers in office buildings.

"Go to I.T.," I reminded myself. "Report John's bloody printer problem. Maybe get some actual answers for a change."

The door to the I.T. room was the only thing I could see clearly, white light shining through the gap at the bottom like a beacon in a sea of black and purple.

I heard that awful feedback screeching before I even opened the door.

The light from screen static hurt my eyes and I flinched away. When I looked back, I wished I hadn't.

Several of their phones were ringing. I couldn't hear them over the terrible shrieking but I saw the handset displays lighting up.

They'd used the rest of their phones to hang themselves.

The room was a forest of dangling limbs and stretched-out cords.

I thought they were dead but I was wrong. They must have sensed my presence, suddenly twitching and stirring, arms and legs jerking violently. It was then I realized the horrible feedback came straight from their throats past their slack blue-lipped mouths.

I slammed the door and recoiled, sweating and shaking and fumbling my way across the thin office carpet. Panic squeezed my lungs as I fled to the stairwell. I had to get someone. I had to get help. My heart thundered and my skull felt like it was in a vice.

The lilac safety lights of the stairwell stared on, unblinking and apathetic, as I tripped and staggered my way down.

It only took three flights to reach my floor but I didn't stop to think about it. Between the fear and the exertion, I was exhausted. My vision tunneled a little and there seemed to be strange sparks in the air. A droning electric hum filled my head and made it hard to think. How did I get so sweaty? Why was I out of breath?

I shook myself. It must be almost lunchtime and I hadn't finished my reports yet. Better get back to it.

The hum in the office was loud. I felt faint. *Just get the reports done and go to lunch. You'll be fine.*

I passed John. He was carving symbols into his flesh with the jagged end of a broken pencil. "Bloody printer," he snarled. I saw his teeth through the holes in his cheeks.

Karen was still humming her little tune while her handset warbled that awful screeching from I.T. She couldn't hear it. She'd cut off her ears. She rolled her eyes at me as I passed and I shrugged.

"Weird," I noted. "Jess is gone. Early lunch?"

"Lunch? It's almost 4pm, mate." Mark didn't look up from what he was doing to admonish me.

I frowned. Was that right? I checked my watch but it had stopped.

Confused, I slumped into my chair and massaged my aching brow. At the back of my mind, something nagged at me, as if I'd forgotten something important.

Darryl heaved again, throwing up all down himself. "I'malrgihh." He still tapped at his keyboard. "I'malrgiiihhhh."

"What..." I struggled. Talking felt like wading through fog. I found it hard to tear my eyes from the screen. "What's the date?"

"28th."

"No..." I murmured. "Can't be." I wiped my mouth, feeling wetness there. I was drooling. The humming sound pressed down on me but I fought to think through it.

A terrible thundering noise, like monstrous hail against the windows, seized my attention. My legs rebelled against standing but I was able to force my way up. Walking to the window was like struggling against a tide. Everything inside me wanted to sit back down, to get back to work. I won out against it, but barely.

Outside, thousands of birds smashed themselves to death against the buildings, rocketing into the ground.

"Something's wrong," I said to myself. I knew, deep in my bones, that I had to hold onto that thought like a life raft. Something was wrong. If I could just keep that thought fixed in place then maybe I could get out of this.

"The I.T. team," I snarled the memory out through a protesting jaw. "Something…happened to the I.T. team."

"Bloody I.T.," growled John. The skin of his forehead was completely gone. He carved symbols into skull bone.

Darryl's desk was coated in his viscous brown vomit but still he tapped his keys.

A bird slammed into the window and I stumbled back in shock, tripping and falling. Jess lay there. I hadn't noticed her before, though I must've stepped right over her. Her skull was the wrong shape. Her hair was matted with bits of it. Dark red clumps flecked the soaking carpet. I looked down. My shoes were wet through with red.

She held a metal hole punch; a tuft of her hair still stuck to it.

I'd been thinking about something important but I could no longer remember what.

I frowned and got back to my feet. My body creaked and my brain felt like I hadn't slept in days. I had a hard time focusing. Still, it was almost time to head home.

I glanced at Paul on my way back to my desk. His face was pressed against the monitor, flesh merged with the screen. His remaining eye rolled around in its socket and he ground his teeth uselessly.

That electric hum gathered around my head like a swarm of flies and I hurried back to sit down, returning to the safety of the lilac menus. I was crying but I didn't know why.

Mark leaned back in his chair to catch my attention. "Lunch?" His eyes were missing.

"Yeah, I could use a break. Must be losing my marbles."

BURNING DAY

The strangest thing about the mornings was the quiet.

Marius remembered that the birds used to be loud in the morning. His parents would be awake already, moving around downstairs, their voices a murmur through the floorboards. There was the sound of the kettle boiling, cupboards, and the fridge being opened and closed. If he was lucky, even the sound of bacon in the pan. Breakfast noises, that's how he thought of them.

Outside his window, there would be other sounds too: engines starting, front doors closing, and gruff 'good mornings' shared by neighbors who had to be on their way. These were the sounds of the street waking up, in the same way a person might arise with a yawn.

All of these sounds were part of the comforting routine of waking, a natural alarm clock that had roused him steadily from slumber. Except for when the birds woke him.

He had never liked the birds. Their shrill whistling and tittering were impossible to sleep through and their harsh, insistent cries were anything but gentle, always jerking him from sleep. Marius would stuff the pillow over his head to drown them out, wishing that a cat would come and chase the raucous creatures away.

Now, as he watched the sunlight bloom slowly across the sky, Marius realized he missed the boisterous music of the birds. There was no one to sing to the sun anymore.

There was no one left at all.

He got out of bed just after the earthquake.

It was only a small one, rattling the windows and the kitchen cupboards. He lay still and waited it out, as he had many times. Something fell over in the downstairs hallway. Probably the hat stand.

When the earthquakes first begun, all the dogs in the neighborhood went berserk. Even Ralphy, the most even-tempered dog in the world, would go mad, running around the house barking and whining. For Marius, that was far scarier than all the shaking and rumbling; seeing gentle Ralphy, the big lazy dog who couldn't be bothered to move even if you sat on him and had never barked in his life, acting like a thing possessed. It frightened him deeply.

Of course, there was no barking outside now.

Once the quake was over, Marius went downstairs. He found the hat stand and righted it near the front door. There were no hats on it. Only his father had ever worn a hat. Marius looked at the stand for a while and wondered what the point of a hat stand with no hat was. Why bother standing it back up again at all? His mother would have wanted the place tidy, he resolved, so he should keep it that way, even if she wasn't here to see it.

Breakfast was cold beans from a tin. There were few tins left in the cupboard, the last of his supply. The local shops had been cleared out over a year ago. Marius raided all the houses in the neighborhood since then. No one was making food anymore but plenty of people left things behind. Marius had been careful with his tins, just as the instructions in his notebook said, rationing himself and keeping little caches hidden around the house in case someone broke in to steal them.

There were gangs who would do that kind of thing. Groups of kids, opting for safety in numbers, taking what they wanted from wherever they could. The Rat Boys were the closest. They lived in several houses by the old play-ground, only a few streets away from Marius's house. They'd offered him a place with them, not long after the Great Burning, but he refused. He wanted to stay in his parents' house and there was something about them he didn't trust. Their leader, Hernan, had a strange look in his eye; something desperate and dangerous all at once.

Marius was glad of the decision two months later when he found a dead boy at the end of his street. The words "Rat Boys Rule" had been spray-painted on his bare torso and his head was smashed in with a brick. He wouldn't have wanted to hurt anyone. Marius always walked the other way when he left the house now and didn't even look in that di-rection. He didn't know if the dead boy was still there. Thankfully, the Rat Boys never came looking for him. Maybe they'd all had their Burning Days by now.

After breakfast, he went for a walk.

He took his rucksack, in case he found anything worth keeping, and carefully locked the door behind him. He wasn't sure why, since anyone could just break the windows, but it made him feel safer.

On the way through the front garden, he patted the top of the little wooden cross that marked the spot where Ralphy was buried and said, "Good boy." Even though he spoke quietly, his voice sounded loud in the stillness.

Outside the gate, he added the full bin bag from the kitchen to the pile that had accumulated there. It ran the full length of the wall now and rested on top of it in places. There was no one to collect it but Marius still felt he should pile it there. It's where the bags had always been placed.

His walk took him to the end of the street and across the main road. He didn't stop to check for cars because there weren't any. All the cars were dead. They went the same day all the batteries died, the power stations went offline, and the phone lines all over the world fell silent.

He crossed the little bridge over the river, past the post office and Bird Bone Lane. The sign called it Little Lane but no one had called it that for a long time. When the adults had still been around, they cleared away all the dead birds from the streets and gardens; but after the Great Burning, there hadn't been many left to finish the job. In the end, the kids shoveled them like some nightmarish snow into Little Lane, so at least they were out of the way.

No one uses Bird Bone Lane now. It was carpeted with tens of thousands of little white bones.

He walked briskly past the burnt-down church, trying not to look at its charred remains. One of the first new commandments had been the destruction of the old, false idols. Marius didn't want to risk upsetting the Deliverer. Not when his Burning Day was so close.

His parents hadn't raised him to be religious but the idea of the Deliverer frightened him. The priests said that He had come to save everyone from the dying of the world and that only through Him could they escape destruction. His parents had been skeptical at first but a lot of people started believing in the Deliverer. Especially when things took a turn for the worse.

Marius's walk took him down to the beach. They'd come here a lot when he was younger. Now the beach was the graveyard of the sea. He smelled the decay a long time before he caught sight of the water. He leaned on the railings at the top of the steps, overlooking the long sandy crescent of the bay. He could barely see the sand beneath the fish. There were remains of every size, from tiny silvery creatures to massive things with giant teeth. Great whales had beached themselves here, in their hundreds, some the size of buses. Now they lay still, their skin peeled away and blubber rotting steadily day by day, slowly revealing the bones beneath with the patience of an archaeologist.

For week after week, the fauna of the sea had thrown itself from the waves to gasp to death on land. The whole beach should have been covered in birds, cawing excitedly over this free and unprecedented meal but the birds killed themselves around the same time, flying headlong into the ground in their millions.

More people turned to the Deliverer after that. Science hadn't explained the earthquakes and couldn't explain the mass animal suicides. People were afraid. The Deliverer offered comfort and, more importantly, promised salvation.

The priests seemed crazy at first. They built no church and created no holy book. All they asked for was that people dig. They gathered followers in their hundreds, then in their thousands, and burrowed into the earth, forcing their way down through mud and stone.

"The Burning Doors are beneath us," they proclaimed. "Through the Burning Doors, we will escape this world!"

They looked insane, with their shaved heads and red shadow painted beneath their eyes. Still, they gained followers by the day.

Mr. Edgar, from next door, had been a religious man his whole life. He dismissed them loudly and frequently as zealots and lunatics.

A volcano erupted in the south and over twenty thousand people died trying to breathe ash.

More followers joined the priests.

Hurricanes tore apart half a city, only a few hours away from where Marius lived. Another fifty thousand dead or trapped without hope of aid. The power station lay in ruins, causing blackouts in neighboring cities too.

The tunnels extended, deeper and faster, with more hands to work them.

The governments of the world met, bringing their top scientific minds together to pool intelligence and pour funding into finding a way to fix it all. A chasm opened up beneath them and the whole city disappeared into the earth. There was no one left to estimate the numbers of the dead.

The next day, the power went out for everyone, for good. Every clock stopped. Every circuit died. There were no more bickering scientists on television because there was no television. Panic became a local thing that could be shared only with those closest to you.

The day after that, there was another earthquake. This was the worst one Marius had ever felt, so bad that Ralphy was inconsolable. He growled and snapped at anyone who tried to come close to him. Marius's parents locked him in the bathroom when Ralphy started frothing at the mouth. His mother shouted at him through the door to cover his ears but he didn't and he heard the awful snarling become full-throated vicious barking. He heard his father shouting at Ralphy to sit, to stay, to stop.

He heard his mother scream and the gunshot half a heartbeat later.

He never saw Ralphy again. His father buried him without letting Marius see the body. His mother wore a bandage on her arm from then until the Great Burning. It bled through often and needed changing, but it was too far to walk to the hospital and the nearest doctor's surgery had been abandoned and looted.

Mr. Edgar came to Ralphy's funeral. He said Marius was lucky. He had passed the Robinsons's home down the street and went inside to check on them when he found their door open. Their dog had 'done for' both of them and disappeared, Mr. Edgar said.

Marius wasn't sure he knew exactly what that meant but there was a bloody implication in Mr. Edgar's tone. Marius couldn't imagine Layla, the Robinsons' dopey labrador, doing anything violent.

The next time Marius saw Mr. Edgar, the elderly man had shaved his head and painted red shadows beneath his eyes. He didn't seem to see Marius. He didn't seem to see anything. He didn't say goodbye.

The neighborhood felt darker after that. People watched one another carefully on the street, scurrying past with paranoid glances. Friends avoided each other and locked their doors at night. Some stopped venturing out at all.

Occasionally, they'd hear a scream or a gunshot, distant but never far away enough. Marius's mother always held him close when such things happened, covering his ears tightly.

He shook himself from past memories and looked out at the graveyard beach, wondering how a whole world could die. There weren't even any insects to disturb the ocean's dead.

With only two days left until his Burning Day, Marius packed up the last tins of food in his rucksack and started the long walk into the city.

The temple to the Deliverer stood on the hill. Inside, he would find the start of the tunnel. There were other temples in other cities, each one sitting atop a pathway down into the ground. Each pathway led to a Burning Door.

That was what had converted the final skeptics. All that time, they had assumed the priests were madmen scrabbling in the dirt, but when they finally found their Burning Doors, hidden beneath the earth, there was no way to deny them anymore. This was proof. The Deliverer was real and he could save them.

What choice did desperate people have?

There were no governments or scientists or specialists anymore. Even if there were, with electronic communication shattered, there was no way for anyone to know about it. There were no space shuttles to take them off the planet. Only one group offered a solution. It was either stay and die or take a leap of faith through a Burning Door.

The rules of the Burning Door were simple enough and Marius recited them over and over as he trudged the dusty pathways into the city, between the rusting corpses of cars. Children could not use the Burning Door. They were too small; not strong enough to survive the touch of the Deliverer.

Even now, Marius remembered the horror that sunk his

heart as he realized his parents would be leaving without him.

Tears ran down his mother's face, leaving tracks in the dust there. "We'll be waiting on the other side, I promise."

"You have to be brave, Marius," his father said, his voice oddly thick. "Keep to yourself. Save what food you can. Don't take chances. I've written down everything you need to do in the notebook on the table."

His father hugged him then, squeezing so hard, it almost hurt. Marius could tell he was trying not to cry, so he did the same. He was terrified but he wanted to show them he could be strong.

"Be safe, my brave, brave boy," his father said.

They'd shaved their heads already. They daubed the red beneath their eyes before leaving and closed the door behind them.

He spent the night inside a bin, carefully climbing in and closing the lid with as little noise as possible. He was scared that someone might find him but he didn't hear a single sound all night. In fact, he hadn't heard a sound that he hadn't made himself for the whole journey. He wondered if he was the last living thing left in the world. The thought didn't make him feel any safer.

He could see the temple on the hill by the afternoon.

It wasn't really a temple, not in the traditional sense. Instead, what marked a place of worship for the Deliverer was the great piles of excavated earth and stone, taller than the buildings around them.

Marius decided to keep walking, even as the sun began to paint longer shadows. He didn't feel safe in the silent city and didn't want to stay another night in an unknown place but, if he could reach the temple, it would all be okay.

After midnight, it would be his Burning Day. He'd be able to go straight through the Burning Door and his parents would be waiting. His heart ached at the thought and he almost started crying with the hurt of longing.

Instead, he put one foot in front of the other, determined to reach the temple before night fell fully. Shadows lengthened around him, long dark fingers cast by tall buildings to ensnare him. He kept walking.

The way to the temple was lined with discarded tools. Mechanical diggers bowed their heads in servitude and picks and shovels lay like forgotten bones along the path.

Marius panted at the entrance. He'd pushed hard to arrive before the sun disappeared completely and he wished he'd stopped to take one last look at it before it sank beneath the horizon. He wouldn't see it again. He wasn't sure where the Deliverer took people, but if it was a different place, it must have a different sky with different stars. Marius wondered if there would be birds singing in the mornings.

There was no altar nor statues. There was only the hole and steps that led down into it; a dark passage down into the earth that would lead him to the Burning Door.

Fear had driven Marius through the silent city, but it gave way to anxiety now that he had arrived. He expected the temple to be welcoming, the gateway to salvation, but it felt just as empty and barren as everywhere else did.

Worse, Marius felt uncertain. What if he didn't shave his head right or got the wrong kind of red for his face? What if he'd counted the days wrong and it wasn't his Burning Day after all? What if he got to the other side and his parents weren't there?

Marius took a few deep and shaking breaths to calm himself. He'd survived a year on his own. He'd been brave like his parents told him and he'd followed their instructions closely. He'd even memorized them, though he still had the notebook. He'd taken no chances in keeping himself safe. He was almost home.

Marius stood up straight, wiped his eyes, and began to descend.

———

Before the Great Burning, someone had laid out oil lamps to help those who would come after. The circular marks their bases had made on the floor stood testament to how many there had once been. There were less than a handful left.

He selected the one that looked in the best condition and lit it with the matches he carried in his rucksack. He was hungry but he didn't want to stop now, not when he was so close, not for any reason. He was proud of himself for having two tins left when he would have needed only one. He had done a good job of saving his food wisely. He hoped his parents would be proud.

The steps that were cut into the dark stone gave way to a smooth slope after a hundred or so. The way was steep and Marius slowed, holding his lamp high to avoid anything that might send him tumbling into the dark. He couldn't imagine anything worse than breaking the lamp and having to feel his way down.

———

He lost track of how long he'd been walking.

His legs ached and sweat ran down his face. He'd given up his fight against hunger hours ago and wolfed down a tin of cold spaghetti. The lamp was still going strong for now but he checked it regularly. He didn't know how long it would last nor how long he still had to walk.

Sweat dripped from his brow and dribbled down his spine and he realized the tunnel was growing warmer.

Soon, the air was uncomfortably close and Marius used the last of his water to wet his cotton-wool mouth.

He was drenched in sweat.

The oil lamp was burning low but he no longer needed it; a dim orange glow provided enough light to see by. An occasional wind rushed up the tunnel, ruffling his hair and pushing against his progress. It came every few minutes with a sibilant roar, stinging his eyes and making his steps clumsy.

Marius's legs were sore and he was tired but he knew he had to be close. He'd be with his parents again soon if he could just complete this last challenge. His parents would look after him, he'd be safe and loved and no longer alone.

The passage downwards turned a corner and Marius was greeted by the cause of the orange glow. It blazed so brightly that he had to shield his eyes from it at first. The heat struck him like he'd just opened an oven.

There, within the rock of the floor, was a great circle of roaring flames, a pool of rippling fire.

The Burning Door.

His heart beat fast and his mouth was dry. All those doubts came worming back out of the dark corners of his mind, holding his arms and legs in place. *What if I counted wrong and it's not my Burning Day? What if something goes wrong? What if it hurts? What if my parents aren't there on the other side?*

The flames writhed with sudden ferocity as a gust of wind blew out from the pool, so strong it knocked Marius back a few paces.

A second later, he felt the tell-tale pre-rumble of an incoming quake. He'd felt enough of them to know this would be a big one. Being deep underground suddenly seemed very dangerous. What if the ceiling collapsed on him? Or trapped him and kept him just out of reach of the Burning Door?

Marius took a deep breath and hurriedly drew out the scissors and the paint from his bag. He had never been more afraid than he was now—not those first nights after the

Great Burning when he'd been alone in the house in the dark, not when he found the corpse of the boy down the road, not when Ralphy went berserk.

If he didn't step through the Burning Door soon, he might lose his chance.

Chunks of rubble fell from the ceiling, smashing on the ground and scattering into gravel as Marius clumsily daubed the red beneath his eyes. He was panting now, crying, his heart hammering while he choked back sobs. On shaking legs, he rose and staggered towards the Burning Door. Another chunk of ceiling fell, stinging his face with shrapnel.

He stared down into the fire, screwed up his eyes, and held the faces of his parents in his mind, hoping with all his might to see them in a moment.

Then he leapt into the Burning Door.

Then he screamed.

The earthquake did not die away this time.

It tore through the continents like paper, pulling down trees and buildings, opening cracks in the land that plunged whole countries into the dark. The seas dropped away as new holes were ripped through the crust and mantle beneath them. Mountains split and spouts of molten rock erupted, hundreds of miles high, painting the sky black with the ash that came with them.

In less than an hour, the dead planet was ripped apart entirely.

In the void of space, the newborn stretched its body, freshly hatched. Grown strong on all it had consumed, it unfurled its wings and let out a hungry cry from thousands of blazing mouths before flying off into the stars in search of its next meal.

IMPOSTER

The plane rumbled again, and Neil grabbed the armrests like they were life rafts.

The occupant of Seat 14F chuckled and shot him a grin. "First time flying?"

Neil did not return the expression. "Not my first time." He prized his fingers free, certain he was going to leave permanent grooves by the end of the flight. "I'm just not a good traveler."

"I used to be like that myself. Unfortunately, I've got no choice. Damn company sends me all over. Won't even pay for business class, the cheapskates. You know what helps?"

Neil did his best to unstiffen his spine with only limited success. He was pretty sure that not being talked at by strangers would probably help a fair bit, but 14F was going to deny him that particular respite.

"Lose yourself."

"Excuse me?" Neil forced his shoulders down and exhaled, but the plane jolted again, and he went right back to throttling the armrests.

"Lose yourself. A book, a movie, music, a podcast—do whatever it takes. Escapism, man. Forget the plane and lose yourself."

Neil had to admit it made sense, but he wasn't sure anything would be distracting enough to make him forget he was thousands of feet in the air. He shot a look at 14H, who had the window seat. She was slumped and snoring against the wall. She'd been that way since hour two of the journey. Every now and then, her leg would twitch out, and she'd kick him. It always seemed to hit him right above the ankle.

"Don't worry, pal," said 14F. "Only fifteen hours to go!"

Neil closed his eyes, gritted his teeth, and tried to pretend he was anywhere else. A still lake. A tranquil forest. A silent mountaintop. Any of the places his therapist had suggested might be calming. They'd never worked before; all Neil seemed to picture were eels, bears, and the frozen corpses on Everest.

He had never been good at relaxing.

The *bing* of the 'fasten seatbelts' light made him jump and he scrambled to buckle the clasp as his life depended on immediate compliance.

"This is your captain speaking. Just letting you know that we're heading into some stormy weather. The ride may get a little more bumpy but it's nothing at all to worry about. For your own safety, please remain seated with your seatbelts on and tray tables in the upright position."

Neil paled, and sweat broke out on his brow.

"Don't worry." A passing stewardess, on patrol to check for unbuckled seatbelts, clearly recognized his distress. "We deal with rough weather all the time. It's nothing to be worried about."

"I told him the exact same thing." 14F gave a winning smile. "I'm James, by the way."

Neil shut his eyes tight. Possibly the only thing worse than being talked at by 14F was having to listen to 14F flirt.

The storm hit hard.

14H was jolted from sleep and shot Neil a dirty look like it was his fault. Neil was too busy fighting his rising gorge to respond. He shook, drenched in sweat. 14F had stopped trying to make conversation and leaned as far away as possible, wary of the potential mess to come.

Thunder rumbled loudly. Every flash of lightning gave Neil palpitations. He knew he was losing it because some of the lights out there looked green.

The next jolt proved too much, and Neil tore off his seatbelt and lurched past 14F into the aisle way.

"Sir!" A stewardess started towards him, but he staggered onward, bursting into the toilet just in time. On his knees, he gripped the plastic bowl and heaved while the lights flickered and the floor lurched.

He wasn't sure how long he spent vomiting, but none of it made him feel much better. He fought to keep steady against the turbulence while he rinsed his mouth and washed his face, but still bumped his head repeatedly against the glass. When he was done, he looked at his pale visage in the mirror. All the lights went out.

Neil was thrown sideways from his feet, and the plane screamed in metal agony. His fall carried him right out of the toilet door and into the aisle way. Someone's blood sprayed across his face. All was chaos. Passengers brawled everywhere, tearing and gouging at each other, frenzied.

Neil knew he was going to die.

The plane jolted Elise awake.

For a second, she thought the guy in 14G had kicked her, and she glared at him, only to recoil in embarrassment as the plane quaked again, and she realized the poor guy had done nothing wrong. Lightning flashed outside, and she flinched away from the window. Had she been having a nightmare? She frowned. She remembered falling out of the plane bathroom. She remembered blood.

"Get a grip," she muttered to herself. It was hardly a surprising thing to have bad dreams, given she was asleep on a plane in a storm. She eyed the black clouds out of the window. Whatever weird glass they used made the lightning look a little green.

The guy in 14G fled his seat to go throw up, and Elise felt

a pang of sympathy for him. This was a hell of a flight to get stuck on with airsickness. She was used to it. Damn company sent her all over. Wouldn't even pay for business class, the cheapskates.

Elise frowned. Where had that thought come from? She worked at a restaurant owned by her parents. She shook herself and put it down to weird leftovers from the nightmare.

"Hey, you okay?"

14F was looking at her, all soft-eyed concern and a half-smile. She felt an immediate, violent dislike towards him. Something deep in her core reacted like this man was her mortal enemy.

"Imposter," she snarled.

"What?" he said.

Then all the lights went out.

Elise tasted blood.

James rolled his eyes as 14G made a break for it. Typical newbie flyer. He turned to watch the desperate bathroom run, mostly just to see if 14G made it or emptied his guts all over the aisle.

In turning, James came face-to-face with the blonde woman in the seat behind, staring at him so intently that he flinched.

Her eyes were wide, and her hair was damp with sweat. "You've got to kill it," she said. "It's in here with us. You've got to kill it before this plane touches down."

Slowly and carefully, James turned back around and sat. *Best not to move too fast and spook the crazy person.* He turned to ask the chick in 14H if she'd heard the mad babbling but found her frowning at him like he was a difficult math problem.

"Hey, you okay?"

"This isn't right," she mumbled. "I killed you already. I solved it. I remember."

"What?"

Then all the lights went out, and James knew he was going to die.

———

Neil rinsed his mouth, washed his face, and studied his pale visage in the mirror. Something was very wrong. He knew it in his bones. The storm rumbled and Neil couldn't help but picture something outside trying to get in, pressing itself against the windows and wrapping around the fuselage.

He shook himself. Being airsick and a little nervous was one thing, but flights of fancy like that were just childish. He imagined his brothers and sisters back at the restaurant laughing at him. Poor little Elise, the youngest one and scared of everything.

He shook himself. Neil. His name was Neil.

He left the bathroom on shaking legs and looked over to his seat. Not far to go and 14F wasn't there. Perfect.

Three passengers had turned around to look at him. Each of them pale and sweating, each of them wide-eyed and bloodshot. He froze under their glares, unsure of what to do.

"It's in here somewhere," said one of them, an older man with thinning hair. "It could be you."

"It is him. It's all of us." A blonde woman with a narrow face.

"She's right. You heard 14H: everyone has to go."

"We tried that already. It's still here."

"I don't have any other ideas." The fat man stood and took off his tie. Then he slipped it over the head of the man next to him and started strangling him.

The cabin erupted into chaos, and Neil fell back as the other passengers launched themselves at each other. An arm wrapped around his neck, cutting off his air.

"You know"—hot breath and a rasping voice in his ear—"I think I was 14G originally. No way of knowing now, though. Did you get my message in the bathroom?"

Neil couldn't answer. The life was choked from him.

Elise leaned back, panting. 14F had put up a fight, but it was over now; she was sure of it. The imposter was gone. The loop was done. The other passengers looked at her in horror, all frozen in place. They'd never know she saved them. It didn't matter so long as the thing didn't make it to the ground. It had spread like wildfire through the plane. If it made it into an airport...

She stood up, still half in a daze from where he'd punched her. Her nose was broken. Her mouth was full of blood, not all hers. There were others who were bloody, too, she realized. A fat man. A narrow-faced woman. A balding guy. Each had attacked someone. Were there other imposters then? And where was Neil? Was she Neil? Or was Neil in the bathroom still? She'd lost her footing in the chain of events.

Elise staggered to the bathroom, stepping over the stewardess, who was still bleeding out. Another imposter? How far had it got?

"Is it over this time?" one of the others asked. "Did we get it?"

"How can we tell?"

"It leaves a trail every time, right? Anyone got any memories that aren't theirs?"

"We haven't reset. Maybe that means it's over?"

"Please don't hurt us," a passenger blurted. "Just let us go."

Elise opened the bathroom door. Neil was in there. He'd gouged out his own throat. In blood on the walls, he'd written *We're lost. It's all of us.* Again and again, he'd written it. They'd written it. Elise remembered writing it when she was Neil.

She turned back to the others. "I don't think we got it. I think it's too late. We all have to go. It's the only way."

The woman was close to tears. "I don't want to. This isn't fair. I have a wife and kid."

"Do you? How do you know they're even yours?" the fat

man asked. "It might have dragged that memory into you from someone else."

"I remember them too," Elise mumbled. She remembered Johnny's first Christmas and Cleo being born.

"Don't you dare," the woman snarled, "don't you dare suggest they aren't mine."

"Every time I looked at it," the other man said, "I had this urge, like an instinct screaming at me. I knew I had to kill it. Anyone getting that from anyone else right now?"

"Every time? How many times have you been around?" asked the fat man.

"Twenty-eight."

"Jesus. I thought I was bad at fifteen."

"Twenty-two," said the woman.

"It doesn't matter," the man insisted. "You killed me first, even though I've been going around longer. Don't you get it? Time is messed up. How many hours left on the flight?"

The fat man checked the nearest display, terrified passengers flinching away from him. "Eight hours."

"It was less than that on my first go-round," said the woman. "It was closer to six."

"Makes no damn sense," said the fat man.

"It's still here," said Elise. "I know it is."

The storm rocked the plane again, and the lights went out. All the other passengers screamed. Something sharp stabbed into the back of Elise's neck, right at the base of the skull.

He was loose in the air. He was falling through the storm. He couldn't survive here. It was killing him. He was coming apart more and more each second. He gripped onto the metal hull. He needed somewhere safe. He needed to live.

In the bathroom, Neil studied his pale visage in the mirror. He looked sad. He looked tired. He looked resigned.

He started to rip at his own throat and used his blood to write the message he would later read. The message he'd already written and had yet to write.

————

James tasted blood.

"It's not me!" The blonde woman gargled her last, and he let her fall. The cabin was a wreck filled with mess and bodies.

He was the last one left. He'd made it. The nightmare was over.

He sagged against the wall and started to laugh until he started to cry. He looked down at hands he didn't recognize, flexing them. Was he 14F or 14G? Or any of the others? Could he be certain? He remembered parents that weren't his and children he didn't have. He remembered his first period and coming round after bypass surgery and the way his wife looked on their wedding night and coming out to his brother. His brain creaked with it all, filled to bursting.

"Who am I?" he asked the dead. "Which one of you am I?"

He knew the answer: all of them and none.

James staggered to the bathroom. His neck felt tight from where he'd been choked to death. Was that the last go-round? Or the one before? Elise had torn his throat out with her teeth. James remembered the feel of his flesh stuck between her molars, from when he'd been Elise.

In the bathroom, Neil's message glared at him from every wall. He finally understood what it meant. We're lost. It's all of us.

If he was the last one left, and he was all of them, then it was him, too.

James sobbed. It wasn't over. It never would be.

He broke the mirror and used the shards to open his wrists.

The plane rumbled again, and Neil grabbed the armrests like they were life rafts.

James chuckled and shot him a grin. "First time flying?"

Neil did not return the expression. "Not my first time." He prized his fingers free, almost certain he was going to leave permanent grooves by the end of the flight. Not that there would be an end of this flight. "Not the first time for any of us."

"No," James agreed. "You know what helps?"

Neil did his best to unstiffen his spine with only limited success. He felt the weight of every time he'd died and every time he'd killed. He'd lost count of both.

"Lose yourself."

"We're already lost."

"Don't worry, pal. Only fifteen hours to go."

Neil nodded and sank his thumbs into James's eyes.

THE SEED

Petey was a smoker. We all had our own thing, really. Josh was into CrossFit—or what we called the Cult of CrossFit to wind him up—and Henry had his charity runs, like the London Marathon the year before. I'd played a bit of rugby in high school and kept myself in shape since. I wasn't a fitness fanatic or anything but I went to the gym a couple of times a week and found some satisfaction in sweat.

Petey didn't play sports anymore, not since the accident. He'd broken his ankle in a high school football game, never bothered with the physio, and the ankle had been weak ever since. He'd been a decent footballer, but his ability came from raw talent, not practice. We used to joke that he was allergic to hard work.

One consequence of all of this was his near-constant complaining since the start of our hiking trip. Another was that he always got up before the rest of us for a morning smoke to "get him going."

So, it was Petey who found the body.

I was awoken by his choking cry of "Fuck!" At first, I just assumed he'd tripped over a guy rope or gotten another splinter or any other of the myriad issues he'd had so far that no one else seemed to suffer from. I elected to ignore it in favor of burrowing deeper into my sleeping bag. The mountain air was bitterly cold in the mornings.

"Guys," he yelled. "You gotta see this! Fucking hell!"

Okay, that sounded serious, but not dangerous. The tone of his voice was more shocked and astounded than troubled, so it seemed unlikely he was being mauled by a bear or something.

By the time I got my kit on and stepped out of my tent, stretching in the cold sunlight, the others were already gathered beside Petey, looking at the ground.

It was a skeleton. Half buried in the mud and moss at the base of a tree.

"I almost pissed on him," said Petey, ash hanging long and limp from the unpuffed cigarette in the corner of his mouth.

"Shit." Josh massaged his knuckles unconsciously. I knew him well enough to know it was a sign of nerves. He'd had a disagreement with a motorcyclist when we were teenagers and threw a punch, knocking the guy on his ass at the cost of a broken knuckle. Josh was pretty proud of the story.

I'd never voiced my opinion; that I thought punching a guy who was wearing a motorcycle helmet was a pretty stupid thing to do.

"What killed him?" he asked nervously.

"No idea." Henry had his thinking face on. He was beanpole thin, with that narrow, wiry look some runners get. His cheeks were hollow, and his eyebrows dark and bushy. He was good at looking serious, and he looked pretty serious now. "He must have been here a long time," he said, frowning at the bones. "There's almost nothing left."

"Shit," Josh repeated. "Do we need to report this or something?"

"Yeah, we probably should," I said. "Mark the spot on the map, Henry. We'll call the cops when we get back to civilization."

Henry didn't answer. He was still frowning.

"Henry?"

"It's weird," he murmured. "Look at the way the tree's grown."

It had a tall but thin trunk, not much wider than the ring of both my hands if I put them together. It had silvery-white bark but I had no idea what kind of tree it was. It didn't look like a birch, and that was the only silver tree I knew. Henry was our nature expert, from his time in the scouts and, later, the military.

"What about it?" I asked.

He pointed. "It's grown up past the spine and out through the ribcage. Like it grew through the bones. But this tree has to have been here longer than the body. Look how tall it is."

"So?" Petey noticed the state of his cigarette and tossed it aside with a *tut*, as though it were its fault and not his. He patted his trousers for the pack, even though he always kept it in his shirt pocket. Another sign of nerves.

"Well, how did that happen?" Henry continued, "If the tree was here first, which it had to be, how did it grow up through the body like that?"

"Maybe he fell out of a plane or something?" Josh suggested. "Impaled himself on it."

Henry scrutinized the tree. "No sign of snapped branches or anything."

"Look, Poirot, can we save the CSI shit for the professionals and just get out of here?" Petey's hands shook a little as he lit his replacement smoke. "I don't want to stick around in case whatever did this is still about."

"This guy's been dead for ages, right, Henry?" I said.

"Probably," he replied. "Could be months, could be years. Body decomposition isn't exactly my area of expertise, though."

"I'm with Petey," said Josh. "Let's pack our shit up and get moving."

The way wasn't too challenging, ranging along the southwest face of the mountain. The ground was at an incline the whole way and choked with crawling roots from the trees clustered at the trail's edge. It was easy to trip if you didn't watch your step.

Henry didn't talk much, leading the way with regular consultations of his map. Normally, he'd point out bits of flora and signs of fauna and tell us all sorts of survival stuff we'd never remember but that he found fascinating. Since the body, though, he'd been locked in permanent frown mode.

Josh and Petey, on the other hand, talked more than usual, though deliberately about anything other than the body. They argued about who had the Christmas number one in 1994 and who was going to die next on *The Walking Dead*. They yammered on about anything and everything. I recognized the tactic—keeping the mind too busy to conjure bad thoughts. Kind of like when you hum a song in the dark so you don't think about what might be lurking unseen but close by. A comfort blanket against the cold hand of dread.

Personally, I couldn't get the body out of my mind. I wondered who they'd been and how long they'd been there. I wondered if someone was still looking for them. I was so lost in my thoughts, I almost bumped into Josh, who'd stopped walking. "What's the hold up?" I asked.

"Don't ask me." Josh looked back and shrugged. "The Chief Scout up there is the one who stopped."

Henry stood in the path, looking up at the trees, his frown deeper than ever. Moss and creepers were prevalent in this part of the forest, every tree painted with that spongy vibrant green and hung with looping vines. It was like the set of some pulpy jungle horror film.

"What's going on, Henry?" I asked. He waved for silence before I'd even finished the sentence.

Petey nudged Josh. "What's got Billy so spooked?" he said in his best Arnie impersonation.

Josh chuckled.

"Will you guys shut up?" said Henry, in a sterner voice than he would usually use.

We fell silent, feeling awkward.

"Nothing," said Henry a few moments later. "There's no sounds of life at all. No birdsong, no insects. I haven't seen any tracks or droppings either."

My throat felt very dry all of a sudden. "What does that mean?"

Henry shook his head but didn't look back at us. "I don't know."

"Well that's creepy as fu—!" Josh's sentence turned into a yelp as he stepped forward. The mossy ground crumbled under his foot and he toppled sideways down the slope.

"Josh!" I started after him as quickly as I could, wary that the ground might be unstable.

Josh tumbled and bounced wildly down the sharp incline, his pack coming off as he was thrown around like a ragdoll, impacting jutting roots and green-stained stones. He flailed, trying to grab hold of anything that would slow his descent but found nothing. Finally, after several bone-crunching seconds, he fell over a ledge and disappeared from view.

We heard a thud a heartbeat or two later.

"Josh!" We rushed as quickly as we dared down the slope and to the edge, fearing the worst.

Henry got there first, holding out an arm in warning and peering down over the lip of mossy ground.

Josh had fallen into some kind of crevasse, a narrow split in the earth, letting light into what appeared to be a small cave. The drop looked about fifteen feet.

He wasn't moving. My heart hammered as I peered down, desperate to see any sign of life.

"Josh!" Henry called. "Josh, can you hear me?!"

With a groan, Josh stirred. His forehead creased with pain and he blinked up at us.

"Talk to us," cried Petey.

"I hate this trip," Josh grumbled.

"Try not to move too much," Henry warned. "Check yourself for any broken bones."

"Are you alright?" I called.

Josh sat up slowly and patted himself down, wincing as he touched his ankle.

"I think my ankle is fucked! Not broken but maybe sprained or something. Also, this may have escaped your notice, but I'm in a fucking hole in the ground! Get me out of here!"

"Can you see another way in?" I asked.

Josh looked around. His face screwed up for a moment and he sneezed. "Something down here is messing with my allergies," he said, wiping his face. "No, there's no daylight or anything."

"Okay," said Henry. "Don't panic. We're coming to get you out." He slung his pack off and produced a length of abseiling rope. He tied the rope around a thick trunk, doing something complicated with knots and carabiners, while Petey and I stood there like a pair of useless lemons. Then he tilted himself over the edge and descended rapidly toward Josh.

Getting him out wasn't so easy. Once Henry had attached him to the rope, it was a matter of manpower to haul Josh out of the pit. It seemed to take hours and at the end of it, we were all exhausted, sweating into our gear, shoulders burning with exertion.

"We need to make camp," Henry said, the first to stop gasping at the air and get back on his feet. "We're all too tired to continue and Josh should rest his ankle for tonight. I don't think it's broken but it's a nasty sprain at the very least."

"Can we pitch up somewhere away from the ominous hole in the ground?" said Petey.

Josh continued poking at his swollen ankle and wincing. "There was nothing down there but a bunch of moss and mushrooms."

Henry pointed to the nearest flat area with a break in the trees. "Over there. Come on. We've got a few hours before it gets dark but we might as well get pitched up and comfortable now."

Most of the wood we found in the forest felt damp but we managed to coax it into burning with some effort.

Henry set his travel kettle boiling for tea. "Don't want to use up too much water," he said, apparently half to himself. "We're going to be moving a lot slower now. Might take us an extra day or two to get out of here."

"Do we need to worry about that?" I asked, dumping my armfuls of newly gathered wood onto the pile and wiping the green-brown stain of it from my hands.

Henry shook his head. "We should be fine, so long as we don't act stupid."

Josh sneezed again. He'd been doing that a lot since he came out of the hole.

"I didn't realize you had allergies," jeered Petey, putting on a nasal voice.

"Just hay fever," muttered Josh, clearly unhappy that his tough guy image was being tarnished. "I don't get it all the time. Just when the pollen count is really high."

I scrutinized him for a moment. His eyes weren't puffy or red and his nose didn't look runny. It didn't look much like hay fever to me but I kept quiet. It wasn't like I had any medical expertise.

Despite the drama of the day, we began to relax as the sun set and we ate our dinner of the weird camping rations that Henry had supplied.

"I think mine is some sort of…beans," I said, squinting at the forkful in the fading light. It wasn't the best but I was so hungry after the stress of the accident that I wolfed it down.

Josh grinned. "I had the meatballs."

We all groaned. Of all the boil-in-a-bag meals Henry had brought, the meatballs were unanimously considered the best.

"I guess it's only fair you get the best meal since you had the worst day," I said diplomatically.

"They're okay." Petey waved a hand dismissively. "But it's still camping food. It's not like a home-cooked meal, is it?"

Josh scoffed. "When was the last time you had a home-cooked meal?"

Petey was a renowned bachelor whose diet consisted

largely of microwavable ready meals and takeaway food—another contributing factor to his slowly expanding gut. "You know what I mean," Petey said over our laughter.

"You want to get yourself a housewife, Petey," said Henry. "You need looking after."

"Ha! No thanks! I don't want to be tied down, old ball and chain and all that. I like freedom, me."

"The freedom to live off kebabs and crisps," grunted Josh.

"Well, what about you, big man?" Petey countered. "Where's your woman to make you dinners?"

Josh sneezed. "I do alright by myself, thanks. Plenty of chicken and rice suits me fine. I'm not into marriage and all that. Kids and stuff."

Henry and I shared a look and an eye-roll. Henry was happily married and I'd been seeing my girlfriend for a few months. I'd always been a more long-term kind of guy.

Josh sneezed again. "Urgh," he groaned. "I think I'm going to turn in, guys."

"Good idea," said Henry. "Get plenty of rest for that ankle and we'll get going again in the morning."

I found it hard to sleep that night.

With all the drama of Josh's fall, I'd forgotten about the skeleton we'd found that morning. Once I was alone in the darkness of my tent, its memory resurfaced, like a body freed from the bottom of a lake, bobbing back up to horrify me. I couldn't stop picturing it—the bleached white bone amid the green moss and ruddy earth, roots wound around and through the limbs as though the tree had grown through the body, ribs pushed apart by the thickening trunk, bones creaking under the tightening grasp of the wood.

It couldn't have happened that way; the body wasn't that old. Trees take a while to grow, don't they? Perhaps the trees around here grew more quickly than normal. Something in the soil, maybe? I'd seen pictures on the internet of tree trunks that had overgrown old road signs or abandoned tools that had been left leaning on them, swallowing them into the wood. Could this be like that?

When I did fall asleep, I had a terrible nightmare. I was washing my hands in my bathroom sink at home. My fingertips were covered in earth but I couldn't get them clean. Outside the small window, the moon was full and huge and I heard it throbbing, like a heartbeat. The louder it throbbed, the harder I scrubbed at my fingers, until I realized the mud was coming out from under my nails, oozing out every time I applied pressure. The heartbeat of the moon grew deafening. It was inside my head, making me feel sick. I sank to my knees and watched as the nails lifted free of my fingers, pushed aside by pale white roots growing from the soil beneath.

I awoke with a start, sweating and breathless. My heart pounded in my ears and, just for a second, I thought I heard a giggle. A childish bleat of laughter from right outside my tent. I held my breath and urged my heart to beat quieter but the sound didn't come again and I dismissed it as a weird echo from the nightmare.

Josh wasn't better after a night's rest.

The first thing he did that morning when emerging from his tent was throw up. Violently.

"Bloody hell, Josh!" Petey was on his second cigarette already. "Are you alright, mate? I guess the meatballs weren't that good after all."

"Shut up, Petey," Josh groaned, wiping his mouth on his sleeve and standing up slowly, like a man whose legs are tired from running. "I feel like crap."

His vomit was thick and milky and looked nothing like the rations he'd eaten the night before. It stood out almost luminous in its whiteness against the reddish-brown earth.

"You look pale," I said, shooting a glance at Henry for a more in-depth medical analysis.

"Let's get you moving," said Frowning Henry. "The quicker we get you back to civilization the better, I think."

He'd been right about what he'd said before; the going was considerably slower. On top of his puking and pallid, sweaty complexion, Josh's ankle wasn't much improved. He was reduced to a hobble, leaning on my shoulder as we weaved our way through the weird silent woods.

Petey's huffed and puffed complaints, which had become a staple of our hiking trip, withered away to nothing under the pressure of the quiet woods. I found myself flinching at the twigs we snapped with our clumsy steps. Every noise we made seemed loud and I feared that the din of our lumbering might attract things lurking in the awful stillness.

The rational part of my mind chided me for this childish silliness but I couldn't help looking around in paranoia, glancing through the maze of wood and moss.

When I saw the man, I almost jumped out of my skin.

"Jesus!" I stumbled back, causing Josh to yell in pain as his weight came down on his bad ankle.

The others turned.

"Christ!" Petey gasped, completing our blasphemy and dropping the cigarette he'd been about to light.

"Hello," called the man, his voice loud in this quiet place. "Sorry! I didn't mean to startle you!"

"Uh…that's okay," I managed, my heart still pounding from the fright.

There were others too, I realized; people stepping out from behind the trees. They looked normal enough, dressed in hiking boots and walking trousers, waterproof jackets and hats. They stared at us, expressions weirdly neutral. Perhaps we'd surprised them as much as they had us.

The only one smiling was the first man. He had a strange look, thinning hair atop a light bulb-shaped head. There was a slightly glazed look to his eyes, which were set slightly too far apart. He was the closest one to us, the apparent leader of their strange expedition.

"We're glad to see you," said Henry, approaching him.

"Name's Henry. Our friend took a bit of a fall and his ankle doesn't look good. Do you know how far it is to the village?"

"Oh, you're a long way off yet, I'm afraid," said the man. His smile never faltered. "That ankle looks bad. Perhaps we can help?"

"Is one of you a doctor?" Henry asked, cocking an eyebrow and sparing a glance for the strange crew. They stood where they had first emerged, still staring blankly, the way a cow might when you walk past its field.

Only the man was animated. "No such luck, I'm afraid." He spread his arms wide in a sudden exaggerated shrug. The abrupt action made me flinch. "But we do have some doctors back at our place. It's not far. We'd be happy to help."

"You…live out here?" I ventured.

He faced me and I immediately wished I hadn't spoken. The way he moved was unsettling; his eyes turned and his head followed a half-second later. The grin stayed in place.

"We do," he said. "A little community of our own. Just a few dozen of us, living off the land. We like it. It's peaceful. This place is very…nurturing."

I shot a worried look at Henry. I wasn't sure about this at all. The guy was giving off a seriously creepy vibe and his crew of blank-faced followers was equally unsettling. I watched Henry weighing it up and I did my best to send my reservations to him mentally, willing him to turn them down.

"That's very kind of you but—"

Josh lurched away from me suddenly, falling to all fours and throwing up some more sticky white vomit.

I turned to help him and flinched away as the man appeared amongst us. I hadn't even heard him move. He laid a hand on Josh's shoulder with a tenderness that should have seemed normal under the circumstances but made my guts squirm. I didn't want this guy touching me at all.

When Josh was done emptying his stomach of the weird pale fluid, the man rolled him onto his back and started undoing the buttons and zips of Josh's jacket. Josh could only lay there groaning.

"Hey, what are you doing?" I said, again shooting a quick look at Henry for support. I was pretty against strange forest people manhandling my obviously sick friend. Henry opened his mouth to back me up but his eyes went wide.

"What the fuck?!" was what he said instead.

I turned back to Josh.

The man had opened his jacket and pulled his t-shirt up to reveal a massively swollen stomach. It looked like he'd swallowed a football whole.

"What—" was the only intelligible word in my gasp.

Petey was more eloquent. "What the fucking fuck is that?!" he yelled.

The man pressed slender fingers around the distended belly and then turned to look up at me. "Mushrooms," he said.

He was still smiling.

"Are you sure this is a good idea?" I murmured to Henry, trying not to be heard.

The weird walkers stayed in a rough circle around us as we moved through the trees, like some sort of honor guard. Or prison guards.

"To be honest, mate, no I'm not," Henry muttered back. "I don't like the look of these people. But I like the look of Josh even less. If they've got some medical supplies or a phone or something, that's his best bet at this point."

"What's wrong with him?"

Henry shot a look back at Josh. The strange people had made a makeshift stretcher for him using sticks and rope, their hands moving to the task as though they'd been in a dream, staring into nothing. They hadn't uttered a word. They hadn't so much as exchanged a look or a gesture with one another.

They carried him now between four of them while he lay

on his back groaning incoherently, his hands on his swollen stomach.

"I have no fucking clue," said Henry. "I've never seen anything like it. We have to get him some help, ASAP."

"Welcome," said the smiling man, who had introduced himself as Malcolm. He was at the head of the group and didn't bother turning around, instead spreading his arms wide in presentation.

Beyond him was a space between the trees around the size of a football field. A dozen houses had been built there and I was actually surprised by the quality of the construction. I'd been expecting mud huts or creepy wooden Evil Dead-style shacks but these looked more like homely little log cabins straight out of a holiday brochure. There were even neatly maintained paths between them, linking them to a central dirt road that ran through the middle. The clearing was ringed by trees with white-silver bark.

It would have been picturesque if it wasn't for the ominous feeling I got from Malcolm and his gang.

"Take him to the doctor," Malcolm instructed his mute hiking buddies, who followed him like an empty-minded herd, smiling all the while.

They complied, carrying Josh's bulk without complaint towards a long bungalow at the other end of the clearing. Josh was beyond speaking. He let out a soft moan every now and then and stroked his hands over his belly.

Malcolm kept walking towards the main cluster of buildings and we followed.

"We should go with him," said Petey, glancing after Josh. "Should we go with him?"

"He will be fine," Malcolm said. "You are free to stay here as long as you like. We have room to spare."

"Can we use a phone?" Henry asked. "We should call ahead to the lodge, let them know what happened and why we're delayed. Don't want them thinking we've gone missing and sending out search parties or something."

"No phone here, I'm afraid," said Malcolm. "No mobile

signal either. We're pretty isolated. We like it that way. Back to nature. Returning to the earth!"

Henry frowned. "Where do you get your medical supplies? Your food?"

"Oh, we go into town when we need to do a supply run. We'd be happy to give you a lift the next time we go."

"When's that?"

Malcolm stopped and spun around to face Henry with such suddenness that I thought he was going to attack him or something. Instead, he just stood there, smiling. "I'll check with our quartermaster," he said. "You have nothing to worry about. We don't get many visitors here. We're happy to have guests."

He turned away again just as abruptly.

"This is our town hall!" He gestured to a large building at the rough center of the clearing. There was an honest-to-God well for water out front. It looked like something out of an old-timey painting.

"And there," he indicated a nearby building. "Is our guest-house. There are rooms available on the second floor. Pick whichever ones you like. We'll prepare some food for you. You must be tired and hungry. If you'll excuse me, I have some business to attend to but, please, make yourselves at home. Look around if you like. Visit your friend."

Without another word, he strode to the front door of the town hall and went inside. We were left standing at the center of this weird settlement. I felt exposed like I was being observed from every window and doorway, though there was no sign of anyone.

"What do you think?" I asked Henry.

"Not sure. Place gives me a weird feeling. I reckon we dump our stuff, check on Josh, and get out of here as soon as possible. I'll take the next ride into town and get proper help."

"I think it looks nice enough," said Petey. "It's got a ski-lodge kind of feel, only without the snow. And if they've got proper food, I'll kiss Malcolm. I'm sick of those weird army rations."

"Come on," I said. "Let's put this stuff down."

"Too right," said Petey. "My shoulders are killing me."

The inside of the guest house featured a large seating area on the ground floor that was half lounge, with armchairs around a fireplace, and half dining hall, with a long table and chairs at the other end. There was no sign of a reception desk, nor anyone to direct us. Several sets of antlers and some weird dreamcatchers decorated the walls but I found no sign of any lampshades made of human skin or necklaces of ears I kept expecting. Maybe I'd watched too many horror films.

We went to the second floor where, as promised, we found a corridor of single bedrooms. In each was a bed, a chest of drawers, and a simple wooden chair. There was no way to lock the doors.

"This bed is actually pretty comfy," called Petey through the open door of his chosen room, between Henry's and mine. "Better than the bloody floor anyway. Might actually get some decent sleep tonight!"

I checked under the bed and each drawer. I wasn't sure what I was looking for, really. Some weird black-magic idol made of sticks? A copy of the Necronomicon? Maybe I was being silly. These people were weird, sure, but they lived alone in the woods. That was bound to make anyone a bit odd. Odd didn't mean evil. They'd been nothing but nice and helpful so far.

"Let's go see Josh," I said, making a decision to, if not lower my guard, then at least be a bit kinder with my judgments.

Malcolm was already in the long bungalow when we arrived.

The interior was surprisingly well-equipped as a medical

facility. A generator out the back provided power for lighting and various machines. Several stretcher beds, actual ones—not made of sticks or something—were separated by curtains. The place smelled clean.

Malcolm was in conversation with a woman when we entered. She was short and sturdy, broad and strong rather than fat. She wore a white uniform with the sleeves rolled up and a stethoscope around her neck.

"How far along?" Malcolm was saying as we walked in. His expression was oddly intense, eyes flashing like jewels in a carved wooden mask.

"A day or so, I'd say," she replied. "You found him in time."

"That is good; I was worried. So, no complications?"

"No, everything should be fine."

Malcolm looked up and saw us, his face quickly breaking back into his usual smile. "Ah and here are his friends," he said. "Josh is in good hands here."

"He's resting at the moment," the woman explained, indicating a set of closed curtains further down the row of beds. "We're giving him some fluids."

"Do you know what's wrong with him?" I asked.

The woman gave me a reassuring smile. "Oh yes, we deal with this a lot, believe me."

"You must be tired and hungry," said Malcolm. "Come, there is nothing more you can do for your friend now. He will receive our best care, believe me."

"What about that supply run?" Henry asked. "When can we go into town?"

"You're in luck." Malcolm grinned a smile as sweet and sticky as poisoned honey. "There's one tomorrow morning."

We hesitated. None of us were keen to leave Josh in the care of these odd strangers but there didn't seem to be much alternative for now.

The moment was broken by the rumble of Petey's stomach. "I am pretty hungry..." he conceded, looking to me for permission to indulge his base needs.

It was then I became aware of the emptiness of my own

stomach. I had skipped breakfast; Josh's morning vomit had done in my appetite and half-carrying him all day had been tough. "Alright," I relented.

"Excellent," said Malcolm.

The food on offer was simple—some bread, some cheese, some fruit—but even I had to admit I enjoyed it as I wolfed it down in the seating area of the guest house. It was nice to have something other than energy bars and the suspicious meat in silver packages Henry had provided.

Petey was particularly vocal about it. "It's not a kebab," he said, "but it's a damn sight better than that stuff we have been eating."

"Well, you can pack the rations next time, Petey," said Henry, a little harsher than he probably intended.

Petey widened his eyes and rolled them, like a child behind the back of a parent that just reprimanded them.

"Sorry, mate. I'm just a bit tense about Josh."

"Don't worry. You can go get help tomorrow, right?"

"Right," Henry grunted. "I'm going to turn in, anyway. Night."

Petey yawned. "I'm going to grab a smoke and then I'll do the same. See you guys in the morning. Hopefully, they've got some bacon or something for breakfast."

Not wanting to sit alone, I made my way to bed too. Sleep was not forthcoming, however, and I lay staring at the ceiling, the small window casting light from outside onto the wall in warped squares. My body ached all over and I was so tired my eyes were throbbing, but I just couldn't drift off.

I wasn't sure how long I'd been lying there when I heard the screaming.

I sat bolt upright in the dark, straining my ears. It was distant, faint enough that, for a moment, I wasn't sure if it was the wind or the night-time screeching of some forest creature. I moved from the bed to the window to try and hear more clearly.

When it came again I was sure—it was a human voice. Whoever it was, they were in agony.

Josh.

I grabbed my boots and rammed them on, staggering into the corridor to get the others. Petey's room was empty. Henry's room was locked. I paused, confused. They hadn't given us keys. How could it be locked? Had Henry got a key and kept quiet about it?

I banged the door and called out, rattling the handle. There was no response. Was it stuck somehow?

I heard the screaming again. There was no time to wait.

I hurried down the stairs and out through the front door into the chill of the night. The screams were louder here. Just as I feared, they were coming from the little bungalow that served as a medical center in this messed up place. The lights were on in its windows.

I sprinted across the dirt and grass and grabbed the door handle, fumbling with hands half-numb from the cold. Locked. I heaved and banged and kicked at the wood but the door wouldn't budge. Josh's screaming was near constant now; he'd only pause to gasp a lungful of air before howling again. I was on the verge of tearing my hair out. These savages were doing something to my friend and I couldn't get to him.

I did the only thing I could do—I ran around to the window and grabbed the ledge, standing on tip-toes to see in.

Josh was on the bed. He was naked, his hands and feet tied to the corners by leather straps. He was pale, shaking and sweating, writhing in torment. His belly was huge now, the skin stretched taut. Around the bed were Malcolm, the doctor, and a few others. The doctor looked concerned, checking instruments, watching them like a hawk. The lackeys were apathetic. They seemed not to notice the man screaming at them. Their movements were dream-like, as though they were in a trance. Malcolm, on the other hand, was excited. His hands were clasped together as though in prayer and he bounced on the balls of his feet. His grin was so wide and fixed that there was drool glistening in the corners of his mouth.

I banged against the window but they either couldn't hear me or didn't care.

Josh's skin started to stretch.

It looked like it was being poked from the inside by small hard points like fingers forced through a plastic bag. The skin split and blood burst out in a torrent.

There were three protrusions, small, brown, and hard, twisted and angular, forcing their way out through the rips they'd made in my friend, dripping gore and seeking the light. They were thin at first, only a few millimeters in girth, but they grew quickly, swelling and stretching from their cores, forking as they did. In a heartbeat, the three small branches were almost a foot long each and had grown smaller twig-like members of their own.

Josh screamed the whole time.

My heart hammered in my ears. My eyes prickled and stung. The scene seemed far away as my vision started to tunnel. What I was watching was impossible.

Malcolm and the others took Josh's body. They slipped the leather straps from his limp wrists and ankles and lifted him from the gurney. One of them knocked the thin mattress askew as they moved. Beneath the mattress was darkness, a box built into the bed-frame below. A box full of earth.

Growing stark white against that brown-black soil were dozens of mushrooms.

The last I saw of Josh, I barely recognized him. His face was frozen, twisted somewhere between agony and ecstasy above the wreck of his abdomen, where flesh hung in tatters from glistening dark branches. They carried him toward the door and out of view.

I swayed on my feet, staggering from the window and across the grass. I had to get away. I had to find the others. I needed to warn them. I couldn't breathe, no matter how much I gasped for air. My tongue felt too dry and my brain too big inside my skull. Beneath my feet the world turned sideways, pitching me into darkness.

In my dream, the moon was big and full and throbbed with a heartbeat that filled my head and made me sweat.

I stood in the woods, the trees around me rendered as solid shadows in the silver light, their dark limbs twisted toward me from all angles. They terrified me to an intensely visceral level. They stood still, reaching for me without moving.

There was a tearing sound that made me shudder and pricked my skin into goosebumps. The dark shadow-bark of the trees flaked away and underneath it was cold, pale skin. Human skin. I saw the hair and the pores, the freckles and the veins beneath. These were flesh-trees. A crippling pain lanced through my middle, right below the belly button.

I sank to my knees and looked in time to see my belly swell. In a matter of seconds, it grew to the size of a football, still growing. A terrible pressure built in my testicles, as though they might burst. I wanted to scream but I couldn't catch my breath.

All around me, the flesh trees shivered, cold and naked beneath the throbbing moon.

I woke with a yell, grabbing my stomach with one arm, the other thrashing in blind panic.

I was back in the bedroom I'd taken in the guest house. It was morning. My shoes were by the bed. The door was closed.

I blinked these details in, bewildered, as my heart rate slowed. It had been a dream. How much of it? Was Josh okay? He must be. What I had seen...it couldn't have been real. That it was some fucked up nightmare was a much more preferable alternative. I swung my legs from the bed, my worried hand moving from my stomach to check my balls, where I'd felt that awful pressure.

I found a cold wet stickiness inside the sheets.

"What the fuck?" I gasped to myself, touching it gingerly with my hand. Pale and viscous, there was no mistaking it. I felt a mixture of utter shame and revulsion. How could a nightmare like that have produced such an effect? A wet dream? I hadn't had one since I was a teenager, and never as a result of something like that.

I got dressed, keen to put it out of my mind as quickly as possible. It was some weird psychological effect of this place, I was sure of it. Nothing to worry about. Certainly not something I was going to bring up with the others. I just needed to get out of here as soon as possible. Maybe I'd go into town with Henry, just to get a taste of normalcy. I honestly felt it would do me a world of good to feel some tarmac under my feet, smell some petrol fumes, and see some awful placid daytime TV drivel.

Petey's door was open, his room empty. Henry's was closed but I didn't check to see if it was locked. It had been locked in the dream. If I tested it now and it was locked, that would mean some of the dream was real. That was not a possibility I was prepared to accept. I put off the test and went downstairs instead, where I glimpsed Petey partaking in his morning smoke outside the open front door.

Relieved to see someone who represented normality, I made a beeline through the empty sitting area towards him, but someone else got there first.

"There's no smoking here," grunted a woman. She was a head shorter than Petey, with long gray hair down to her hips. She was carrying a covered basket under one arm, supporting the bottom with the other hand.

"Oh, sorry," said Petey. "I'll move further from the door. Is this your place? It's nice."

"No smoking," the woman snarled, fixing him with a glare as hard as granite. Her lips curled into a snarl.

"Yeah, I get it," said Petey, backing away so he was further from the woman and the door but making no move to extinguish the cigarette. "Sorry, it won't happen again."

In a heartbeat, she dropped the basket and advanced on him, shoulders low, fists out at her sides, mouth locked in a tooth-bearing snarl. "No smoking here," she screamed.

"Jesus!" Petey backed further away in shock.

I made it to the door and stepped out, mouth open to try and diffuse the situation. I stopped dead when I saw what had spilled from the basket.

Mushrooms.

Pale white, standing out against the bare earth and green grass. Freshly picked, by the look of them, with large caps and thick stems.

"Oh dear, oh dear, Moira," said Malcolm, appearing from somewhere. "Come now, let's leave our guests alone."

Moira shot Petey one last growl and gathered up the mushrooms, stuffing them in the basket and storming into the guest house.

"I'm so sorry about that," said Malcolm, his grin entirely insincere. "The poor woman hasn't been quite the same since her husband passed last year. She is quite right, though: I'm afraid we don't allow smoking in the village."

Petey's face twisted in an undisguised mixture of disgust and disbelief. "What? At all?"

"I'm afraid so." Malcolm tilted his head to the side, adding an extra level of creepiness to his constant grin. "It's bad for the trees, you see."

"Did the supply run leave already?" I cut in.

"Ah, yes," said Malcolm, not turning to face me. "I regret that your friend missed it."

I frowned and my mind went straight to the locked bedroom from my nightmare. Had they locked Henry in? Had they done something to him? "I want to see Josh," I said.

"I'm afraid that won't be possible."

"What do you mean?" Petey asked. "Is he okay?"

"He took a turn for the worse in the night," said Malcolm, still grinning as though this wasn't grave news. "He is under close observation and not up for visitors."

"I want to see him," I said firmly.

Malcolm turned to me but said nothing. His eyes gleamed.

I stormed back into the house. It was obvious this grinning lunatic wouldn't let me see Josh but I could definitely see Henry, even if I had to break the door down. He'd never call his weird mute lackeys in time to stop me.

When I reached Henry's door it wasn't locked at all; it swung open too hard as I twisted the handle and put my shoulder to it.

Henry lay in bed, his brow damp with sweat, his dark hair saturated. He was white as the sheet beneath him and he murmured nonsense. Down the side of the mattress and across the dark floorboards, that strange pale vomit congealed in pools.

"Oh Jesus," I whispered.

I approached him slowly, the visions of Josh's belly and the twigs bursting from it fresh in my mind.

Henry had kicked the sheets off in the night, so I saw his stomach hadn't swollen. Not yet. I knew in my bones that it was only a matter of time.

With a shaking hand, I lifted the corner of the thin mattress. Beneath it was a bed of dark, damp earth, and there, drinking the sweat of my friend, were the mushrooms.

I don't remember grabbing Henry and hauling him from the bed, keeping one of his arms across my shoulders. I just knew we had to get out as soon as possible. These people were poisoning us somehow, that was what it was.

"Petey!" I struggled down the stairs. "We've got to leave!"

The other truth this brought home was that I hadn't been dreaming about Josh. It had been real. I'd seen the mushrooms beneath his bed when they'd moved him and now the mushrooms under Henry's mattress…it couldn't be a coincidence. I couldn't explain what I'd seen, I didn't know how it was possible, but I knew it was real.

We had to get out.

I practically hauled Henry down the stairs. He'd been the

fittest of all of us before this, but now he was nearly dead-weight, barely managing to shove his feet along in a shambling mockery of walking.

"Petey," I yelled. I looked everywhere, head-snapping back and forth for any sign of Malcolm or his creepy friends. We were getting out. They'd try to stop us, I knew that. But at least there was no sign of an ambush in the sitting area.

I yelled for Petey again, shoving my way through the door and outside.

Petey appeared around the corner, quickly hiding another cigarette. "What now?" He sounded irritable but his face went white when he saw Henry. "Jesus, what happened to him? Was it the food?"

"Poisoned somehow," I huffed. "We have to get out of here now!"

The urgency in my voice compelled Petey into action and he took Henry's other shoulder and helped me shift him. A line of drool fell from Henry's lips, his eyes unfocused. He mumbled something unintelligible.

"We should get Josh," said Petey. "Are we going back into the woods? Won't we need our stuff?"

"No time," I said, steering us towards the line of silver-white trees.

"What about Josh?"

"He's dead," I said, through gritted teeth. Pin-pricks made my eyes water.

"W-what?"

"He's dead, Petey," I snarled. "The bloody mushrooms did him in and now they're going to do for Henry if we don't get help! And these nutters are all in on it!"

As if summoned, people appeared from the buildings in the weird little village, filing out through the doors. I expected them to rush us, to drag us down and carry us back. They easily out-numbered us and, half-carrying Henry as we were, they'd catch us easily. But they didn't.

Instead, they stood like statues, their faces blank as they watched us struggle towards the tree line.

I risked a glance over my shoulder at them just as a

breeze picked up. In unison, eyes half closed as though in a trance, they swayed with the wind. We were maybe fifty meters away but I heard the susurrus they made with their gaping mouths. It sounded like wind through tree branches.

I shuddered and turned away, dragging Henry faster.

"Josh," Petey mumbled on the other side of Henry's half-limp form. "H-he's dead? When? How? When did you find out?"

"I saw him last night." I expected to sound angry and bitter, but my voice came out hollow. "I thought it was a dream but now I know it wasn't. They weren't treating him at all. They were helping the poison along. His...his stomach..."

I couldn't finish the sentence. The image of Josh came back to me, strapped to the gurney while his bloated stomach was ripped through with twisting wooden limbs, the impossible speed of their growth making them look like wriggling tentacles. I forced the thoughts away and focused on the tree line. Nearly there. If we could get into the forest maybe we could hide. There had to be a road somewhere if these people went on supply runs into the nearest town. We could get away. We could get help for Henry and justice for Josh. The police would come. Everything would be alright.

"What do you mean, his stomach?" Petey's voice was shrill with fear. "What about his stomach?"

We broke into the tree line and, before I could work out how to reply, something snagged on my boot-lace and I tripped. Hobbling together as we were, we all went down, rolling across the root-knotted ground. I reached down to tear away whatever foliage had snared me and get back up as quickly as possible.

I recoiled immediately at the sensation of skin. Skin...and a fingernail.

It wasn't some stray root or fallen twig that had hooked my laces at all. It was a hand. Pale and half-buried in earth, frozen in a claw-like grip.

As though in slow motion, my gaze followed the path of the arm. The rest of the body was just as pale, standing out against the rich, dark earth. The head was mostly buried; I could see only dirty blonde hair and the peak of a nose from my position on the ground. The chest lay open, ribs bent out and snapped with the force of the tree that had grown out from inside the abdomen. A silver-white tree.

I turned as the realization hit, scanning the ground at the base of the trees surrounding the village. Every hoary wooden pillar had a grizzly scene at its base. Some of the bodies were older than others, their bones falling apart. Others still had flesh, still had muscle enough around their faces to display their frozen screams. There must have been hundreds, each buried in the shallow earth sprawling with roots, like twisted wooden hands pinning them down.

"Oh Christ," said Petey, getting back to his knees before following my gaze. "Oh, what the fuck—"

If there was an end to his sentence, I never heard it. Something hard knocked the light out of my eyes.

Waking up was painful.

My eyes burned and my head throbbed violently. The pain, centered somewhere at the back, echoed around the inside of my skull. My mouth was dry. I felt sick and dizzy. I tried to force my eyes open again, reaching to wipe away the tears and shield them from the glare but my wrists were bound. Panicking, I kicked out. My legs were bound too.

After finally blinking away the light, I looked around. Dread settled deep in my stomach as I did.

The row of beds, the gently humming equipment, the smell of disinfectant. The window where I saw what happened to Josh. What was going to happen to me. I was in that damn medical hut.

Henry was on the bed to my left. His straps were loose enough that he could sit up and, I discovered now that I wasn't thrashing blindly, mine were the same. His stomach was swollen and he cradled it like a deep pain. Or a newborn.

"Henry?" I croaked through the desert of my throat.

"He's not really talking much," said a voice to my left. Petey was on the bed there. Dried blood matted his hair on one side, dark and crusty. I reached up to my own throbbing wound. I was clean, bandaged. *Why treat me and not him?*

He lay on his back, staring at the ceiling, almost serene. "Never thought I'd die like this," he said. "Guess I didn't really put much thought into dying at all, really. Murdered by tree-huggers is kind of a curveball though."

I frowned. "Are you okay?" He didn't sound like Petey. He didn't look at me.

"Sorry, mate," he said. "Think the blow to the head did something to me. That and being forced to face my own mortality. Turns out there's a weird kind of calm on the other side of pants-pissing terror."

"We can get out of this," I said without much conviction. I didn't see how. We were tied up in the middle of some woods, who knew how far away from civilization.

"I still don't really know what 'this' is. But it's not my problem for much longer. That bastard Malcolm told me they're going to execute me soon. I'm not good enough to carry the seed apparently. Can't say I'm too broken up about it." He met my eyes for the first time since I'd woken up.

I saw pain there, sorrow, and worst of all, pity.

"Doesn't sound so good for you guys, though," he said.

I turned back to Henry, still cradling himself. He muttered under his breath, repeating something over and over that I couldn't quite make out.

I took another look around the room, testing my bonds again for any sign of weakness but knowing there wouldn't be. I thought about the hundreds of trees planted around the little village, each grown out through a skeleton. I wondered how many people had been in this exact bed before they'd ended up out there. I wondered if the first skeleton we'd found before we even met Malcolm, had been someone who had gotten away only to die alone out in the woods, ripped open from the inside.

With a grim expectancy and a shaking hand, I reached

under the thin mattress beneath me. There was damp earth there, just as I knew there would be. I pulled my hand back and stared dispassionately at the mushroom I'd found. It was like looking at a death sentence. Was I infected already? There was no way to tell.

In a sudden rage, I hurled the little white mushroom against the wall, the leather strap at my wrist audibly snapping tight from the action. The movement abruptly exhausted me and sweat broke out on my brow as my wounded head silently thundered beneath the bandage. The room spun.

I didn't remember going to sleep but I woke myself up by being sick.

There was none of the acidic burn of normal vomit. Instead, the substance I heaved onto the floor was thick and slimy, like mucus. I felt dizzy as I leaned over the edge of the bed and emptied my guts onto the floor. Someone had turned off the lights at some point, which only added to my nausea and disorientation. The only illumination came through the window.

I felt so drained. My breathing was hard, ragged. My heart pounded like I'd run up a hill. All I could do was flop back on the bed and lie in the dark.

Petey, if he was awake, was silent. Henry still whispered to himself.

I watched him, etched out of shadows by moonlight like one of those drawings people make after scratching away the black layer to reveal the silver underneath.

As my heartbeat slowed, I caught the barest breath of his mad utterances.

"My baby, my baby, my baby," he whispered in the dark.

The next day, Henry's stomach was the size of a beach ball.

The doctor, whom I'd come to mentally re-label as "the midwife," declared him ready. Just as they had with Josh, people gathered around the bed. They blocked my view of Henry totally and I wasn't sure if I wanted to struggle to see or not. Malcolm stood at the foot of the bed, his eyes fixed intently on Henry. His grin was intense, stretched tight into corners.

I could barely move, constantly dizzy, constantly nauseous. Even if I hadn't been tied down, I doubted I could do anything to get away from the screaming.

When it was over, I caught a brief glimpse of Henry's face as they carried him past my bed and out the door. His eyes were screwed up tight, tears filling the creases. His mouth was open wide and, in between the screams, he was laughing with pure joy.

The midwife came to me later, hours after Henry was gone.

She pressed a cool hand to my forehead and wiped away my vomit with soft, moist towels. She spoke to me all the while, her voice tender and comforting, though I couldn't really understand what she was saying. Everything seemed like it was coming to me through a tunnel, or maybe through water. My senses were dulled, my head swam. She took my hands and pressed them against my own stomach where I felt the signs of growth.

My throbbing headache carried through into my dream.

The moon was there again, huge, filling almost the whole sky and shining with a light so bright it hurt my eyes. I squeezed them shut but the headache persisted and I felt something move inside my skull, like a twitch in my gray matter. Panic filled me as I scrabbled with my eyes closed.

Something was in my head; some parasite, some invasive being.

It twitched again, a nauseating feeling and a hideous agony as that most vital of inner flesh was forced apart. I coughed and thick, white mucus dribbled from my nose and mouth. Pressure built behind my eyes and the thing moved again, the pain driving me into uncontrolled convulsions on the floor, my fingers clawing gouges in the supple earth.

I knew what it was then. Not some malicious creature at all but a life I nurtured inside myself. It was trapped inside my skull and needed to get out, like a chick stuck within the egg. Despite the pain, I forced my eyes open. I had to help it. It was vital, it was precious, it needed to live.

By the light of the moon, my hands sought out a rock and with all the strength I could muster, I slammed it into my forehead. Once, twice, three times, each with a sickening crack. I felt the thing respond, moving towards the weakness I'd created. I felt its wooden tendrils slither behind my eyes, pushing one of them aside as it sought the moonlight, sprouting out through the socket. More of them continued the work I'd started, thrusting through the cracks I'd made in the bone of my skull, forcing their way free. So strong, so brave. I was filled with an overwhelming sense of pride so powerful, I thought my heart would burst.

This was the life I had carried and now was the moment of birth.

The questing sprouts grew thicker, drinking deep on the light of the moon, pushing my face and forehead apart like shoots through a bulb. All I could do was lie there and cry with pride at the wonderful miracle.

I woke to Petey's screams as they dragged him from the bed.

"You fucking cowards," he roared, thrashing as hard as he could. There were too many of them and they held him firm, apathetic to his fury. "Let me go! I'll fucking fight you! Let me fucking go, you motherfuckers!"

I was nauseous, the room spinning and I could make only garbled mumbling sounds and move my arms weakly.

He saw Malcolm standing passively by, smiling his little smile, as always. Petey practically threw himself at the man, but he couldn't break free. "You fucking bastard! You creepy fucking snake! I'll rip you in half, mate! I'll tear your goddamn head off!"

They carried Petey by all four limbs out through the door and across the grass. I could still see him through the window.

One of them hit him with a hammer right in the back of the head. I heard the crunch from my bed. His shouting stopped and they let him flop to the ground. His legs thrashed, trying to stand with only a damaged brain to guide them. The hammer came down again and again until the legs stopped moving. Malcolm's people stilled for a moment, swaying in unison to a non-existent breeze. Their strange wind-whistle song floated in through the open door.

Poor Petey. I felt sorry for him. It must have been so hard finding out that he wasn't worthy, that his body was too damaged by smoking and neglect to do what Josh, Henry, and I could do. It was hard to feel sad about his death as I rested a hand on my swollen belly. My time would come soon and that was all that mattered. I knew I'd been afraid before, but I could no longer remember why. I could no longer really remember what fear was like.

As I stroked the globe of my stomach, I cried tears of utter joy.

LULLABY

I woke up curled around my bump before I remembered it wasn't there anymore.

My head pounded and bile rose in my throat. The numbers on my alarm clock were too bright. I reached to turn them away but knocked the clock to the floor instead. It clinked against bottles.

I cleared the gunk from my throat but that turned into a coughing fit and soon, I was retching. My lungs felt full of scratchy loft insulation. My eyes stung with burning water and my throat felt like it was cracking. A panic attack would hit me soon if I didn't get air.

A piece of broken glass pierced my heel as I staggered to the window. Breathing was the bigger concern for the moment, so I ignored it and hobbled the rest of the way, fumbling the latch and sliding it open.

The freezing breeze hit me and I dry heaved into the quiet of the night-time streets. Nothing came up but sticky drool. I spat it into the yard and wiped the back of my hand across sore lips. My watering eyes gave the streetlights a haze, the sky still a deep black with no sign of dawn. I pressed my fingers to my temples to try and ease off the headache.

When did the yard get into such a state? There was grass poking up through the flagstones and the hedge hadn't been trimmed for months. I was sure Mike had been out there working the other day.

The memory was like a punch in the gut.

Mike had left. Right after waking was the easiest time to forget. Some days, it was all I thought about. I'd wander from room to room, chasing his ghost, trying to remember the times we had before it all fell apart. It was harder and harder to picture being happy. The echoes of angry words lingered throughout the house, caked into the wallpaper, layered across the furniture like thick dust waiting to be disturbed so it could rise into the air and choke me. Every day, they got louder.

I was still sweating despite the bitter cold. My hands shook. I needed a drink to calm down and then a nice, long sleep. There had to be a bottle here somewhere with something left in it. I turned back to the musty room to look for one.

The lullaby stopped me in my tracks.

Only a few notes, softly sung but clear, as if the singer was just outside the open window behind me. My lip quivered. A trick of a half-asleep mind still saturated with booze, it had to be.

I took a few shaking breaths. *Find some drink, find some medicine, go to sleep.* I couldn't make my legs move; my bare feet felt frozen to the boards. I needed to look.

Powerless as though on marionette strings, I turned back to the window.

An involuntary cry escaped my mouth and my hand went up to quiet it. Bile rose again in my throat.

There was an empty stroller in the street.

I squinted through still-watering eyes, trying to find some reason to disbelieve. I knew that stroller. I knew the little daisies patterned on it and I knew how the handles felt, even though I'd never gotten to use it properly. I'd practiced with it up and down the hall while Mike was at work.

It sat directly beneath the street light, angled towards the front gate.

This wasn't happening. This was an episode of some

kind. I was having another breakdown. I had to find something real and cling to it for dear life until the storm passed. *Mike. I should call Mike.*

I'd taken one step back towards the bed when I heard the next few notes of the lullaby. They were sung softly, and my heart was hammering loud, but I was certain.

"No," I whimpered and thrashed away, sending bottles rolling. There was no one there. Sweat beaded on my brow and poured down my ribs, sticking my shirt to me. No one else knew that tune. I'd made it up myself, a lilting string of notes with no words attached. I'd sung it to the bump every night and resolved to sing it every night after the baby came.

I couldn't turn back to the window. I couldn't stand the idea that I might see the stroller had somehow moved closer, that it was now in the yard or by the front door.

With a burst of frantic energy, I rushed for the bed, childhood instinct drawing me to the blanket for protection. I forgot about the broken glass on the floor. I went down with a sharp cry and a thud as more slid into my bare feet. I groped at them in the dark and my fingers came away warm and wet.

The lullaby called again.

I screamed, grabbing my face with my hands, smearing the blood on my cheeks.

My scream choked into a new fit of coughing, a rasping, hacking, wretched noise. Tears ran down my face and my bloody feet throbbed. I had to get my phone. *Call Mike. Call an ambulance. Call anyone.*

I checked the bedside table and the floor around it. The charger cable lay unused. I must have left the phone downstairs. That meant venturing into the darkness of the house to find it. The thought filled me with a quivering dread. In here, I had the medicine and drink and sleep. Out there, memories waited to ambush me. I wasn't safe outside this room.

I couldn't stay here either. I'd go mad with fright if the lullaby kept assaulting me. *Find the phone.* Mike would help. He had to. He still loved me.

I crawled around to the door, my feet still bleeding freely. Each breath came out with a whimper at the end of it and the tears kept flowing. I tried to take some deep breaths and steel myself but breathing too deeply threatened to start me coughing again. I had to make do with some quick rabbit breaths before gritting my teeth and yanking the handle down.

Across the silent hallway, the wedding photo leered at me. I was overcome with such a hatred for the woman in the photograph that I forgot my fear for a moment. She was young and happy, full of optimism and bright plans for the future. I scrambled to the photo, ignoring the pain in my feet and the bloody marks my hands made on the walls. I ripped it from the hook and hurled it down the stairs with a noise that was half snarl, half sob.

The lullaby came again, louder than before, filling my head with the next few notes of the song I'd made. I clamped my hands over my ears and fell to my knees, body racked by sobbing. I could see down into the hall from this position.

The front door was wide open. The hallway was bathed in streetlight and icy cold. Whatever was doing this to me, it had broken in already. I wasn't safe.

"No, no, no, no, no," I whispered desperately. I tried to make for the stairs as the panic attack finally hit. *Just get to the phone. Just call Mike.* My head swam. I couldn't raise a gasp through my closed throat. As my vision started to tunnel, I remembered I couldn't call Mike if I wanted to. He'd blocked my number, telling me he wouldn't speak to me again unless I got help.

The lullaby was louder than ever in my ears but I couldn't find the breath to scream.

It was my voice singing.

"Hypothermia," the paramedic grunted.

"Really?" The other was younger and less experienced. "Indoors?"

"It happens with addicts sometimes. They're out of it, they leave all the doors and windows open. They don't realize how cold it is. This time of year is a killer."

"You think she just lay down and died at the top of the stairs?"

"Or passed out. Was probably here for hours before someone noticed the front door open and called us. Look, her keys were still in the lock. Sounds like the TV is still on too."

"She looks so afraid."

"Try not to think about it, lad. Get the stretcher and let's get her out of here, eh?"

"I'll go switch off the TV."

"Don't touch anything. Police might still want to poke around."

"I just want to look—oh god."

"What is it?"

"It's not the TV! It's her! Looks like a recording of herself singing. My sister did one of these when she was expecting so she could play it back to the baby."

"Go get the stretcher, lad. Move that buggy out of the way too. Can't believe people 'round here, just leaving their rubbish in the street like that."

CHANGES

We all feel it the day the forest changes.

It's something hard to describe but easy to perceive. The dogs are unsettled. Trees that surrounded us our whole lives, familiar as family members, suddenly seem threatening. The darkness between them is deeper.

As always, in times of uncertainty, villagers consult the Wise Woman for advice.

"From inside the mountain. Older than old." She will say no more about it. She double-checks all the charms around her house, feathers in place and bones still hanging in their proper order, known only to her.

Strange noises permeate the night, sounds that not even my uncle can identify. People shutter their windows as though it were storm season.

"Do not concern yourself with it," my uncle tells me, though I catch him glaring out into the woods. "Whatever their fate is, we will be exempt. You must focus on your change now."

We will be gone once my change comes. That is the way of my kind.

Supplies begin to dwindle and food is carefully rationed. Something has driven away the animals. Fruit withers on the vine. The villagers rely on my uncle to find game, more than ever before. That is part of the unspoken condition of our life among them; we use our skills to provide.

I don't remember my parents—my uncle has always been my guardian. Everyone is wary of him. He is gruff, isolated, and quiet, but I know his attitude isn't the real reason for the distance between him and the rest of the village. People are cautious of him by instinct alone. There is no hostility, merely an understanding that my uncle and I are *other*. We are different. The way we understand each other without speaking, the way of the predator about us, the change that takes our kind; these are the things that separate us from them.

I inherited some of that distance, though not as great. I am young and harmless, so most people pay me no mind. I am even allowed to play with their children, though my uncle shackles me with certain rules that they do not have.

"Do not go near the dogs," he forbids.

I disobeyed him once, drawn by curiosity and the desire to join other children. They played with the animals often. My uncle was right: the dogs did not like me. I learned a sharp red lesson that day and did not go near them again.

The older men of the village had more sense than to try to punish me for the incident but the younger men were angry. They were concerned I had upset the dogs and their children might have been hurt in the scuffle. They sought to punish me as they would a child, with beating and berating.

I am not a child like theirs.

My uncle drove them from our home with blazing eyes and told them in a thundering voice, "Remember who I am and what that means!"

They did not trouble us again.

A hunting party went missing. Their delay was expected; they had been forced further into the forest in search of game.

After several days, however, people started to worry.

After six days, one of their number returns. He is covered in blood, none of it his, and he refuses to say a word. He chews up his own tongue and falls into a kind of sleep from which he cannot be awoken. His eyes are open the whole time. He stares at nothing. Some people believe he went mad and murdered the others. Where else did the blood come from? Others want to go after the rest of the party, hoping to find them, or at least recover their bodies.

The Wise Woman says, "It's too late for them. It's too late for us all." It is the last thing she ever says. The man is left in her care.

I have unsettling dreams. I know my change is coming soon and my uncle warned me these feverish nightmares would be part of it. In the night, I shiver. My bones burn and my skin stings.

I also dream of chanting in the trees, harsh voices hissing, but I don't know if that is normal or not. My uncle keeps careful watch over me. He is nervous for me but tries not to show it.

Awake, my senses sharpen.

The village women act strangely. They are withdrawn, sullen, aggressive. Even my best friend has fallen under this affliction. She says nothing and walks away when I call to her. When I reach for her, she scowls at me fiercely and I recoil. Perhaps this is part of my change. Perhaps the distance between myself and other people will increase now and they will treat me as they treat my uncle.

A man argues with his wife in the dusty street. She is disrespectful to him, he tells her. Her attitude is unacceptable. He grabs her arm when she tries to walk away. She wheels around to face him with vicious speed, her face a feral snarl. At the same moment, all birdsong stops, and every other woman freezes too, dropping what they are doing in unison to glare at the man. Their eyes, and hers, are so full of hatred. The man releases her, casting her arm away as though it were a hot pan and stumbling back. The women return to their business in silence.

The birds never start singing again.

No one dares go hunting. They beg my uncle to go for them but he refuses to leave me alone. He is impatient now, his body thrumming with the energy of it, waiting for my change. He does not sleep at night but stands guard over me instead.

The food stores are almost empty until one night, someone kills all the hunting dogs. We do not know if it was one of the villagers, out of hunger, or something else. Either way, the meat is eaten. People are desperate.

The women seclude themselves. They speak only to each other and only ever in whispers. They share glances across the street, like unspoken secrets.

The men of the village play a game. They throw a ball and score points. I know this is a last stand against desperation; a last chance to pretend everything is happy. People are determined to have fun, to take their minds off the looming dread of the forest. Even my uncle and I are invited to join.

"It will be good for your muscles," my uncle says, to my surprise. An even greater shock is when he joins in.

I don't know the rules of the game and it does not matter. Only the action is important, the defiance of terror. Men leap in extravagant dives to catch this ball, rolling across the dirt, as though to let it fall would mean death.

In the end, we collapse in the grass, exhausted and sweating. Immediately, I know something is wrong. I hear the chanting from my dreams but I am not asleep. I know my uncle hears it too—he raises his head and frowns deeply —but the others cannot. I recognize the voices of the village women.

I start to run. They are gathered somewhere close. I know I must reach them.

The sun drops from the sky, careening below the mountains, plunging us into a sudden unnatural night. My skin stings. My bones burn. My breath comes out as steam. The change is on me.

I'm running on all fours.

The Wise Woman is dead, her body laid at the center of the village. Her charms are broken and tossed around her, some clutched in her fingers, their strings knotted about her knuckles. Her skin is covered with muddy handprints from head to toe but it doesn't look like any violence was done to her. She is strangely peaceful.

The chanting is louder now. I see glimpses of the women, gray shapes fleeing my approach, vanishing into the woods like ghosts. One of them is left behind in the street. She has been ripped into chunks that tremble in the mud. Her severed head still lives, eyes bulging, tongue lapping at her own blood.

The change has overcome me completely. My uncle has followed me, taking his true shape, too. I want to chase the women, to help my friend. My uncle makes a whining noise from his throat, warning me against it. He paws the ground and shakes his head. *We can go. We can leave them now. In the end, we were never truly a part of these people. Their fate does not have to be ours.*

I don't know what to do.

I howl at the fleeting shapes.

PARASITE

I saw my reflection blink.

People talk about fear being a cold sensation; icy dread, goose-bumps and a chill up the spine. For me, fear was hot, clammy, and claustrophobic. Whenever I got really scared, my neck and forehead would sweat and my body felt like it ran a fever.

This fear hit me like stepping into a sauna.

I wanted to look away, but the cords of my neck had turned to iron so I just stared at my own sweaty face in the mirror, terrified that something else might happen.

Several minutes passed in slow silence and I began to push the fear aside and look at it logically, like my dad had taught me.

As a kid, I'd been afraid of everything. Spiders, bugs, snakes, dogs, strangers, the woods, and especially the dark. Every night, I had to have the light on and, every night, I'd hide under my blanket anyway. As soon as it got dark, I'd avoid looking through any windows, just in case I saw something terrible looking back.

My family home was an old farmhouse in the country, seated in a bay of trees before a sea of rolling fields. The woods at night were full of creaking trees, the haunting hoots of owls and foxes shrieking like murder victims. The outside of the house was scattered with wind-chimes and dream-catchers because my mum was an ex-hippy and liked that kind of thing. Every time I heard them jingle in the dark, it sent me into fits of terror.

Don't even get me started on the cellar, which was dark even with the light on, and full of thick webs and thicker shadows.

One day, my dad sat me down and gave me a long talk about logic and the value of applying it to these fears.

"When you get scared," he said, "your imagination runs wild. It conjures up all kinds of monsters. That's the curse of being a creative person. But if you force yourself to stop and think about it, take a deep breath, and analyze the situation, you'll see there's nothing there to be scared of."

It had taken a long time for me to get the hang of it but one day, it just clicked into place. I realized that the wind-chimes were just blowing in the breeze, the owls and the foxes were just hungry, and that the night held exactly the same things as the day did. I wasn't afraid anymore. I hadn't really been afraid since.

I was now.

I took a deep breath and applied the iron tools of logic to the situation.

I could have imagined the whole thing. I was tired. Work was stressful and I hadn't been sleeping well. My bathroom light had developed an occasional flicker, the herald of a dying bulb. It seemed plausible that I had been tricked by a tired mind and a brief shadow.

My pulse began to slow as I took deep breaths and scrutinized my reflection. There was nothing strange there. Why had I been so afraid anyway? Sure, an independently blinking reflection was weird, but the abject terror I'd experienced seemed an over-the-top reaction in hindsight.

I mentally put the whole thing to one side and brushed my teeth, although I'd be lying if I said I didn't avoid looking in the mirror while I did. Just in case.

It wasn't long before my mind was back on work and all the things I had to get done in the day ahead. There was a big deadline coming up and no one else in my team seemed to be pulling their weight. No matter how much work I got done, there was always more to do.

In the shower, the mental checklist of tasks took my full attention, so much so that I suddenly realized I'd been in there far too long. I wrenched the water off and shoved the curtain aside, almost tripping over the side of the tub as I grabbed for a towel. I shot a look at the mirror, feeling weirdly smug that it was now covered in condensation so I couldn't see my reflection anymore. *Can't blink weirdly at me now, can you?*

Then I saw the message.

It wasn't new, that much I was certain of. It hadn't been drawn in the condensation but highlighted by it, the edges of the finger-tracks standing out across the glass. An old message but one I knew I hadn't put there.

Who are you?

That was what someone had written on the mirror in my bathroom.

On the way to work, I realized it must have been Rob. He'd crashed at my place last weekend and he'd taken a shower then. It still seemed like a strange thing to write; I would have expected an insult or a picture of a penis from him, but maybe it hadn't been meant for me to see it. Maybe Rob had strange moments of introspection after showers that could only be aided by questions posed in condensation.

By the time I got to work, the stressed mental list-making had already taken back control of my conscious mind and I forgot all about the mirror and its parade of morning weirdness.

I woke up screaming at three the following morning.

It was one of those bolt-upright awakenings accompanied by a throaty yell. Fading after-images clung to my eyes, projecting themselves against the darkness of my bedroom like a light show on smoke.

I hit the light in panic, nearly knocking over the lamp. The fear of the nightmare was dissipating, but I still scrutinized each corner of the room, checking for boogeymen. When I was sure there was no immediate danger, I sat and listened for a while, trying to force my sense of hearing to permeate the walls of my apartment to the living room, the kitchen, in case anything was lurking there.

I heard nothing but the occasional click of the heating and I was long used to that sound; I hated being cold.

I was coated in sweat, but I covered myself back up with the blankets anyway, clinging to the night-time armor of a child. I couldn't even remember what the nightmare was about.

It took me a while to get back to sleep and when I did, it was with the light still on.

***

It happened again the next three nights in a row.

It wasn't always the same time. Sometimes it was only an hour after I'd fallen asleep, sometimes it was just before I had to get up, but each time I was drenched in sweat and panting hard. Each time I'd completely forgotten what the nightmare was about.

"You need to keep a dream diary by the bed," Janine advised between bites of her sandwich.

I'd led us to a quiet corner of the office cafeteria to seek out her and Rob's advice on the matter.

I gave her a skeptical look. Mum may have been a hippy but none of that stuff got passed down to me.

"I'm serious." She continued to crunch mouthfuls of celery and bread. "I'm not saying you have to interpret your dreams or anything wishy-washy but there's obviously something bothering you."

"Yeah, but I don't remember it," I replied.

"Hence: journal. As soon as you wake up, you need to

grab a pen and start writing. It doesn't matter if it's gobbledygook or just random words, it might give you a hint about whatever's upsetting you so much."

"Not a tough thing to figure out." Rob opened his second packet of crisps. He layered them into his own sandwich with the care of an artisan. "It's this place. I've told you a thousand times, you can't take work-stress home with you."

"How can I not? It's okay for you guys, you don't work with a bunch of lazy morons. You've got teams that have functional members. I'm basically carrying my team and they couldn't care less."

"Find a way to relax, man," Rob said. "I'm serious. You're going to burn yourself out. Hell, try the dream journal idea, it might make you feel better."

After two more nights of nightmares, I gave in and bought a notebook and pen to put by the bed. I treated it to a wary look, as though warning it not to get any ideas about my belief in its abilities but, secretly, I hoped it helped. Anything was better than more nightmares.

When I woke up the next morning, I was so used to the nightmares that I couldn't remember if I'd had one or not. Cautiously, like checking under a stone for a spider, I flipped open the first page. To my surprise, there was writing there.

"Who are you?" it said.

I debated with myself all morning about whether to show Rob and Janine. I'd brought the notebook with me to work. It was only small, a slim lined pad with a plain black cover, but I felt the weight of it in my bag, as though the words inside were heavy.

In the end, I was too freaked out to keep it to myself. At least having witnesses would confirm it was real and not some imagined prop in a rapidly developing psychosis.

"Are you kidding?" Was Rob's response, holding up the damning evidence. "You're telling me you wrote this in your sleep?"

"I'm telling you I didn't write it at all." I turned my face away from the words and burrowed deeper into my jumper, despite the sweat on my brow. "At least, I don't remember writing it."

"Well, I've heard of sleep-walking, sleep-talking, and even sleep-eating, but I have never heard of someone sleep-writing."

"Maybe you woke up, wrote it, and went back to sleep," Janine suggested. "I packed two lunches for Hank yesterday because I wasn't fully awake. I have no memory of packing the first one."

"Maybe." It was good to have something logical to cling to. "But why those words? It's a bit weird isn't it?"

"I think Rob's right," said Janine. "You're stressed out and it's affecting your sleep, that much is clear. But maybe it's also raising some issues for you. You're not happy here. This is your subconscious reaching out, posing a relevant question to you."

Rob rolled his eyes. "Maybe you should get an aura reading."

Janine didn't rise to the bait. "The subconscious is serious business. You should try writing a question of your own in the book and see if Half-Asleep-You replies."

The idea sent a shiver down my spine. I wasn't entirely sure I wanted to open up lines of communication with whatever had written the words, even if it was me. Every horror movie I'd ever seen suggested that was a bad idea. Then again, the paranoid part of my mind had already raised the subject of demonic possession, ghosts, and all sorts of other supernatural culprits. The subconscious mind reaching out through sleep was a welcome alternative because it was a shade closer to recognized science. Maybe my subconscious just wanted me to quit my job and go on a gap year to Tibet or something.

It wasn't much for logic, but it had to be better than

weird mirrors and nightmare diaries. It had to be better than waking up screaming every night.

That night, my reflection blinked again.

I was trying to shave without looking in the mirror, which was proving difficult to say the least. When I finally gave up, took a deep breath, and met my own eyes, they blinked.

I'd spent so long building up wall after wall of rationale after the first time, convincing myself it hadn't happened. Seeing it happen again broke all those defenses instantly.

Worse, this time I saw something in the eyes of my reflection before they blinked: a glint of utter hatred. It was only there for a split second, but the expression was unmistakable.

In that moment, there was no doubt in my mind that the entity in the mirror wanted to do me harm.

I fled from the room, slamming the door and leaning against it with my hands, breathing hard. I was braced to keep it closed but if I actually felt something push against the other side of the door, I would lose my mind with fright.

What the hell was happening? Why was it happening to me? What had I done to deserve this?

The sweat of fear dripped from my face, hitting my bare feet in spatters. Was I going mad? I had to be going mad. It was the only thing that made sense. The only other option was that the world had gone mad instead.

I retreated to my bedroom, leaving all the lights on behind me and making sure the door was firmly closed. I turned the TV up loud so there was no way I would hear anything outside my room. If there were things creeping through my apartment to get me, I didn't want to hear them. I'd much rather deny their existence until the last possible moment.

After an hour, I had calmed down enough to stop looking for any sign of a turn in the bedroom door handle.

I was tired, but sleep was the province of nightmares, so I forced myself awake with mindless browsing on my phone.

It wasn't long before my morbid fascination led me down the path of folklore research. I knew it was a bad idea. I knew it would just give fuel to my imagination. I looked it up anyway.

In two hours, I learned more about superstitions surrounding mirrors than I had ever known existed. Everyone seemed to have beliefs about them, from the ancient Romans and Chinese to early American slaves. None of them were good.

Some said a mirror could trap a wandering dreamer so they should be covered at night. Some said that souls could be locked in mirrors, cursed to be stuck behind glass forever. Others said that a mirror could show the reflections of any entities in your home, living or dead. I shivered as I read the warning: once you've seen them, they become aware of you too.

That ship had certainly sailed. Shivering, I added another blanket to the bed and crawled under the pile.

I woke up screaming again.

I flailed in panic and banged my heel on something hard. My back hurt and I was so, so cold. As my waking mind raced to add up what my senses were telling it, I realized it was too bright in there. Was I late for work?

I blinked and looked around.

My heart stopped beating in my chest. I was in the bathroom. I'd woken up in the bathroom, directly beneath the mirror.

I jerked as though I'd been electrocuted and flung myself towards the door, shoving it open and slamming it behind me before staggering across the hallway to the opposite wall.

I felt sick and shaky, and the cold of the bathroom floor clung to me. That frigid numbness felt somehow familiar and terrifying, as though something in me recognized it and recoiled instinctively.

How did I get in there? I'd fallen asleep in bed. Had I got up to use the bathroom and collapsed?

Had something carried me there?

The thought made me shudder to the depths of my spine.

The alarm sounded from my bedroom and I jumped out of my skin. I had to get ready for work.

"I'm getting seriously worried about you, buddy," said Rob, in between mouthfuls of club sandwich. On Fridays, we ate lunch at a little pub around the corner. "You look terrible."

"First sleep-writing and now sleep-walking." Janine poked at her salad. "Obviously something is seriously disturbing you."

"Let me book you an appointment with my doctor," Rob said. "He can see you first thing in the morning."

"I'm not sure a doctor can help," I said numbly. Sounds had a weird echo to them, and it took effort to drag my gaze around, like my eyes had partly rusted in their sockets. I could still feel the cold of the bathroom floor on my skin, in my bones.

"You're wearing two coats and a jumper but you're still sweating," Rob insisted. "It's definitely time for a doctor. This'll all be down to diet or stress or something, you'll see."

"And you still don't remember the nightmares at all?" Janine asked.

I frowned hard. "I remember a kid. Sat on a wall at the beach. I'm behind them. They haven't seen me. They've got red shorts. Blonde hair. I remember feeling so cold. Impossibly cold."

I shuddered while Rob and Janine exchanged a worried glance.

"What you need is rest." Janine laid a hand on my forearm and I jerked away in surprise. Her hands felt burning hot.

"You see?" she said. "You're wound up. On edge. Why don't you go visit your folks? They live in the country, right?"

I nodded vaguely. "Maybe." *It might do me some good,* I considered. *Get away for the weekend. Have some home cooking. Feel safe.*

"Doctors first," said Rob. "I'm going to make you an appointment right now."

He finished his last mouthful and stood, fishing his phone out of his pocket and moving to a quieter area to make the call.

I looked over at him but caught sight of the mirror behind the bar and quickly looked away again. Logic said I wouldn't be able to see my reflection from where I was sitting. Imagination said I'd see it anyway.

"Did you hear me?" Janine asked softly.

"Sorry?" I mumbled.

"That's okay, I don't blame you, you're clearly exhausted. I said, have you checked the dream journal? Maybe you wrote something before you went walkabout."

I shuddered with horror at the thought.

I knew I hadn't packed the journal. I'd been in such a rush to flee my apartment that I'd just grabbed my bag, my keys, and my wallet and headed out the door. I'd taken the journal out of my bag when I got home yesterday, so there was no way it could be in there now.

I knew it would be anyway.

Dread filled my stomach like a creeping mist, spreading out from the pit of my gut. I pulled out the book and the pages flopped open in my hand. The writing was all over the paper, written at every angle. Numbly, I turned a page. And another. And another.

Get Out.

Get Out was what it said. Over and over again.

I stood up, head spinning. The floor lurched beneath me. Janine said something but it came through fractured, like an echo in a deep cave. The lights began to flicker, just like the ones in my apartment. I forced my legs to move. I couldn't stay here. I had to get away.

I made it to my car and slammed the door behind me. There, in the little metal box with the windows up, I tried desperately to catch my breath. My hands gripped the steering wheel hard, knuckles like pale pink jewels set in ivory skin. Sweat dripped from my face.

I didn't want to go home to where the mirror waited. I didn't want to go anywhere. I just wanted the whole world outside my car to disappear.

I didn't remember making the decision to drive to my parents' place. Maybe it was Janine's suggestion or maybe it was the only place I could think of where I might feel safe. I wasn't a nostalgic person. In fact, I didn't have many memories of my childhood—everything before the age of seven was kind of a blur—but I knew I could always find security and safety at that house.

My phone buzzed. A text from Rob. *We'll cover for you at work. Get some rest. Call if you need anything.*

I breathed a little easier. Somewhere in the Higher Function Department of my brain, some middle manager of logic was satisfied that I could leave without losing my job.

I didn't look at my bag on the passenger seat. I didn't remember bringing it. In fact, I was pretty sure I had left it in the pub. I knew the journal was in there, with all its nightmare words.

I started the car and tried not to look at the mirrors. Was that my intense expression or someone else's looking back? I didn't know anymore.

My parents were surprised and a little concerned when I showed up unannounced late that afternoon looking pale and stressed. They were pleased to see me and they gave me hugs and cups of tea, but there was worry behind their smiles. I told them I'd taken some time off work and I hadn't seen them in so long that I wanted to visit.

In familiar surroundings, I was much calmer. I went back to telling myself that it was stress, that it was a breakdown, that I just needed a few days of rest and relaxation. Country air and home cooking. It was an easy medication to prescribe myself.

My old room was how I left it. Posters of action movies on the wall, a dusty collection of young adult books on the shelf, and piles of VHS tapes by the little portable TV I'd been given for my twelfth birthday. It was strange and a little awkward that my parents kept it that way, the way someone mourning the tragic loss of a child might. I was only a few hours away by car, after all.

Thankfully, there were no mirrors in my room. There were a few photos of me, though; a little blond kid on a skateboard or halfway up a tree. I chuckled to myself and ran a hand through my—now dark—hair. Where did I go wrong? From carefree kid to stressed-out adult.

I flopped down on the bed, letting familiar sights and smells envelop me like a security blanket.

I woke up to a sharp knock on my bedroom door.

"Dinner's ready," my mother called from the other side.

Instantly, I went into a panic. Was I in danger? Had anything been moved? Had *I* been moved? Nothing was out of place in the room. There was no mysterious writing anywhere, no journal by the bed—I'd made a point of leaving it in the car. Maybe it was finally over.

I let out a relieved breath. This was the first nightmare-less sleep I'd had in days and I felt much better for it.

"Coming," I called.

The kitchen smelled wonderful. Mum had made a roast dinner, complete with homemade gravy. I sat in the same seat I always had and rearranged the cutlery around my plate with a small smile. Dad always forgot I was left-handed. It was a comfort to know that some things never changed.

The talk at dinner was nostalgic but I expected that. The older they got, the more obsessed they became with talking about my childhood. I put it down to standard parent reminiscence and played along, although I couldn't remember a lot of what they were talking about.

They always came back to this supposed family holiday to Fairsands. It was a caravan park down by the beach where the family had a rusty old static. I knew I'd never been to it but, as always, Dad was insistent we'd taken a trip there when I was seven. He seemed almost desperate to get me to acknowledge that this event had actually taken place, concerned eyes searching my face for any hint of recognition.

I nodded and pretended to recall it, just to stop him from getting upset.

That night the wind-chimes around the house were loud and I heard foxes crying out, but I managed to get to sleep anyway.

I woke with a start at 3 a.m. My heart was pounding so hard, it was painful and I was sticky with sweat. I didn't cry out, but I did bolt upright. In the dark of my room, I was sure someone was watching me. I sensed a presence close by. The air was heavy with tense expectation.

Something inside me couldn't take it anymore.

I stormed into the bathroom. I was afraid, but days and days of fear had taken me right to the end of my rope, so I was also furious.

I yanked the pull-chord for the light, almost slammed the bathroom door, and shoved the lock into place before gripping the sink hard with both hands and leaning forward to stare into the mirror.

The mirror's fury matched my own.

Huge dark bags like bruises under my eyes. Pale, sweaty skin and bloodshot eyeballs. The mouth curled into a hateful grimace and I wasn't sure if I was doing it or not.

"I know you're in there," I said.

"I know you're in there," it said.

"I know you're not me," I said.

"I know you're not me," it said.

The lights flickered and made me jump. They were only out for a second but when they came back on, there was writing on the mirror.

Look in the book.

I knew, without looking, that the journal would be on the bathroom chair. I could feel it there, like the edge of a bad dream after waking. My hands trembled but I forced myself to pick it up. I couldn't go on like this. I had to finish it.

I flicked past the *Who are you?*s and the *Get out*s until I found a new entry.

I know you're not me.

The lights flickered again and a new sentence joined it on the page.

Give it back.

Give what back? I didn't understand. This wasn't like some film where I'd stolen some trinket from a mysterious old crone or taken cursed silver from a windy castle.

"I don't understand," I muttered to myself.

"I don't understand," I said to the mirror.

The lights flickered.

You stole it from me.

"Stole what?" I asked, exasperated. "I don't even know who you are! What did I steal from you?"

This time when the lights came back on, the writing was everywhere. It filled the page and spilled out onto the bathroom walls. One word over and over, terrible and furious.

EVERYTHING.

I could feel the anger behind the message like thunder in the air. It bore down on me, an awful pressure and I crumpled to my knees. The lights continued to flicker.

You stole it.

You stole my whole life.

But you can't get rid of me.

Now I'm coming to take it back.

Get out.

I looked at the pen in my hand and a small voice in what was left of my rational mind asked a question: If you blink and you don't realize you're blinking, wouldn't it look like the lights were flickering?

The pain in my head was as sudden as a car crash. It slammed me to the floor and pinned me there under an anvil of hurt. I couldn't see. I couldn't think. Everything behind my eyes was spinning lights and weird sparks as the neurons in my brain lit up like a Christmas tree of agony.

I wrestled one eye open. There was a message on the skirting board.

Get out, you parasite. I'm taking back my body.

The pain came on stronger and I was forced to close my eyes again.

Suddenly, I remembered the nightmare in all its detail.

There was a boy, sitting on a wall. He was kicking his heels against the stone and grains of sand were falling from his shoes onto the beach below. His father had moved away to buy an ice cream from the van nearby. He was alone.

I felt cold. So cold it was like winter in my bones. I couldn't remember what warmth was. The sun's rays couldn't touch me. I cast no shadow.

The boy was facing away, looking out to sea. I felt the warmth in him from where I was. I heard the life gushing in his veins. I wanted to reach out and touch him.

There was no one else around. The people outside their static caravans weren't paying attention to the boy. I was so cold. I could be warm like him. I wanted so much to be warm again, to feel the sun, to wear skin. To feel anything but cold, just for a little while. I'd give it back after a little while.

I couldn't see my own hands as I reached out to stroke his blonde hair.

I woke up in bed with a yawn and a stretch. It was one of those glorious awakenings where everything feels just right and you start the day with a smile on your face. Sunlight was streaming through the windows and I could tell already it was going to be a beautiful day. Perhaps we'd go for a walk down to the river or up the old hiking path. Or maybe we'd go into the village and stop off at the ice cream parlor. I missed the taste of ice cream. I just wanted to do everything. I hadn't been outside in years.

I knew when I went to the bathroom that there wouldn't be any writing on the walls. I knew that was all over with now. I smiled to myself and hummed a little tune as I brushed my teeth. The mirror did nothing unexpected and I met the eyes of my reflection without fear.

I went to breakfast with a smile still on my face and greeted my parents so heartily, they almost jumped.

Dad had made bacon and eggs and doled them out onto my plate straight from the pan.

I picked up my fork in my right hand and started to eat. It felt good to be home.

DRAUGR

The cows were the first sign. We found them at the foot of the cliff, a pile of broken bones and crushed meat. The whole herd had flung themselves over the edge in the night. One was alive, struggling, eyes rolling, until Uncle Olaf brought his hammer down.

"What does it mean?" I asked my father.

He said nothing.

"Wolves didn't do this," Olaf grunted. Father glared at him and the big man fell silent.

Later, back at the house, I listened to the rain and wondered what could have frightened the herd like that. My mother's scream broke me from my thoughts. She shrank back from the window, clutching her face in horror. It wasn't rain at all, but birds. They were dropping dead from the sky.

After that, the adults held a meeting that none of us children were allowed to attend. Still, the word was on everyone's lips and we heard it soon enough.

Draugr.

"What will we do?" my mother asked after I'd been sent to bed.

"I don't know." My father spoke the words with tension in his throat, like a man confessing a crime and hating himself for it. He'd always known how to protect us. His uncertainty was a crime he was ashamed to admit.

"You do know, boy," Grandmother croaked in her old dry voice. "You remember the tales I told you. There's no stopping a thing like that. Greed and hunger are all it knows. It'll destroy all of us if we stay here. Nightmares and madness, blood and slaughter. We have to leave."

"And go where? The other clans will rob and kill us as soon as look at us."

"That's better than what will happen to us if we stay."

The room was quiet after that. I got no sleep that night.

"What is a Draugr, Grandmother?" I waited until my mother and father were out to ask her.

"An evil thing, child. A dead man that won't die, possessed of terrible powers and terrible hunger. For flesh and for wealth."

"A dead man?"

"Yes. Remember Ivar Haraldsen, who was thrown by his horse last year? It'll be him, mark my words. He was a greedy man in life. Just so in death. A Draugr covets wealth most of all. The grave of Ivar Haraldsen is empty of all but stolen gold by night, I'll bet my last teeth on it."

"Is there really no way to stop it?"

"The stories vary. A hero of stout heart, removing the head, burning the body. Forcing it back into its grave before the dawn. Foolish goals. If you're faced with it, make an offering of gold or silver and it may spare you. But running is better."

That night, a terrible flayed bull rampaged through the town. Its bellowing voice was the worst thing I'd ever heard as it left a trail of blood wherever it ran. Anyone who met its eyes was driven mad and fell to writhing and twitching on the ground.

Uncle Olaf went out to stop it with his hammer but it ran him down and trampled him. In the end, he was just as crumpled and broken as the herd that went over the cliff.

We didn't dare retrieve his body until the sun was high above the horizon.

"I'm taking my family and leaving." Frode, the smith, came to tell my father. "We'll be gone before nightfall."

"Where will you go?"

"Anywhere but here."

"You'll be on foot," Rollo reported, coming over to join us. He was very pale, his hands shaking. "I just came from the stables. The horses are all dead. They were eaten. Great pieces of them missing. Gods, the tooth marks were huge, like nothing I've seen."

"I'll wait here no longer." Frode was pale now too. "On foot or crawling if we have to, we're getting out."

It was barely past noon when the sky darkened again. Night hadn't fallen, there were no clouds, but the sunlight strained to reach us and the air turned cold. Mist rolled in from the sea, blanketing the ground, and closing us off from the world.

We were at the long hall tending to the afflicted, who were still writhing and sweating from their encounter with the bull.

My father lit a torch. "Back to the house." One hand was always on his sword now and he snarled at the mist as though it were a creeping snake.

"What about them?" I lowered the moist cloth from the head of Anja, my cousin. She murmured in delirium.

My father glanced back at the stricken people only once. "Leave them."

He pushed me out into the cold, his grip painful on my shoulder. We were only a few steps away when he suddenly seized me and dragged me around a wall, clamping a hand over my mouth.

Something huge moved in the fog. Its steps were heavy, enough to shake the ground. I held my breath and screwed my eyes shut. I didn't want to see.

The dreadful thudding neared and suddenly my father hefted me up and ran. Behind us, screaming started. I couldn't help opening my eyes. Over my father's shoulder, I saw a huge figure in the mist, tearing its way into the long hall. The people inside had nowhere to run.

I heard it laughing and I knew then that we would all die.

The darkness receded again only when the long hall had been completely devastated.

None had been left alive. Only scraps of flesh and bone remained, scattered amongst the ruins in the returning daylight. There wasn't even enough to bury.

More people wanted to leave then until they found Frode and his family strung up in the trees at the edge of the woods. They had been flayed from head to waist, their skin spread across the branches around them in ragged, dripping sheets. The message was clear: there would be no escape.

"We should have run before, while we still could," Grandmother said. "Before it grew too strong."

There were eight men left and my father led them to the burial mound. There had been a Haraldsen in the town as long as anyone could remember and Ivar had been laid to rest with his wealth in a great ship, all of it buried beside the mounds of his ancestors.

The men brought swords and oil. They planned to find Ivar and set his body aflame, then hack it apart. I should not have followed them but I had to see the deed done with my own eyes. The Draugr was a nightmare I would never wake up from unless I knew for certain it was gone.

I crept from shadow to shadow in the dying light, on the way up the hill to the place of the dead. I clutched my mother's silver necklace, stolen from the box beneath the bed. Hunger was what drove the monster, Grandmother had said. For flesh and for wealth.

"He will be sleeping, won't he?" Rollo's quivering voice carried back to me.

"We hope," my father rumbled.

Gorm kept looking over his shoulder, scanning the trees and the sky. "After a meal like that, he should be."

"Careful how you speak. I had family there."

"We all had family there, Rollo."

"Quiet, both of you. We're here."

Even from where I hid, I could see that the tombs of the Haraldsens were broken open, the earth messily furrowed by massive hands and inhuman strength. Ivar's mound was the last along the row and the stones that marked its edges were blackened and cracked, as though struck by lightning.

"He's not here," grunted Gorm. "But look at that pile of gold."

Rollo huffed out a breath. "Not here. Thank the gods, but if not here then where?"

"He took the grave gifts from his own family."

"And from others. That ring was my wife's."

"Don't!"

But Rollo stepped past the circle of broken stones, reaching for the ring.

The Draugr didn't break the ground when it emerged. It simply rose through the hard earth like it was water. Its flesh was pale blue-white but for its hands, which were frostbitten black. With each, it seized a man's head and, with an easy squeeze, turned them to pulp.

The men stood no chance. They threw themselves at the Draugr but their swords left no marks on its skin. Within seconds, they were all gone. My father's limp stump slid, bitten in half, into the open grave.

Nose and mouth caked in blood, the Draugr sniffed the air. Its massive head rolled on its shoulders and those dead eyes found me in my hiding place.

I couldn't move as it approached. I wanted to run but I knew it would catch me. There was nothing left to do. My shaking hands found my mother's necklace and as the Draugr loomed over me, I raised it.

It paused.

"An offering?" Its eyes gleamed. Its breath stank of bile and the fresh kill. For a moment, it considered me, amused. "Very well, boy. The others are mine, but you may go. Do not try to take anyone with you. You leave alone."

It took the necklace and sank back into the ground with a ripple.

In the stillness, I heard the near-distant sounds of the village. My mother called for me.

On shaking legs, I turned away and started walking.

THE UNSEEN

"Jesus Christ, kid!"

I pulled him away from the curb. The horn blared, loud and indignant as the bus roared past. Passengers glared out the window, shaking their heads. None of their kids saw anything. They stared milky-eyed into space, as usual.

"You've got to be more careful!" I took him by the shoulders and gave him a little 'wake up' shake.

His brow creased slightly. "I'm sorry." He seemed genuinely contrite. "I didn't see it."

I looked into his mist-filled eyes and grimaced. "Of course you didn't," I scolded, but only softly. "That's why you have to wait for me to tell you when to cross."

"There was a gap." He pointed at the road. "There still is."

"But not in the traffic," I said. "That bus would have squashed you flat. And then where would I be?"

The lights changed.

"We still good?"

He nodded and chewed at his knuckle a bit.

"Come on then."

We crossed the road. I didn't need to wonder what it must be like not to see the danger in the world. I knew already.

Work was pretty standard: I tapped away at my spreadsheets, and the kid entertained himself with his coloring book. I wondered why he could see that but not cars, computers, or anything remotely technological. If it had moving parts, it was invisible to him. Where was the line? Was the ball in a biro too much? What about a can-opener? When I got my new watch for Christmas and showed it to him, he only stared blankly at me. As far as he could tell, my wrist was bare.

I shuddered. Thinking about stuff like that was a good way to go crazy.

Commotion in the office diverted my attention.

"Oh, god," someone shouted over and over. Panic did embarrassing things to the male voice.

I peeked over the divider separating my desk from Smith's.

Addams was running down the length of the office, clearly frantic. His shirt had come untucked and he was white as a dead man, sweat glistening on his scalp beneath greasy strands of graying hair.

"Where's my kid?" He wrung his hands. "Has anyone seen my kid? Oh, Jesus! God, help me!"

Nobody helped. There was something unspoken in the air, a silent social stepping-back from Addams. A funeral bell tolled in everyone's mind. I heard Smith counting under his breath.

"There you are!" The stricken man threw himself at the little blonde girl by the window. He gripped her savagely by her gray-clad shoulders. "Are you crazy?" he demanded. "What the hell is wrong with you? I could have died!"

She stared up at him with that same look they always have—as though they're half in a dream-world, as though they're not sure if you're real or not.

"You wanna put in for a replacement, Addams," Michaels jeered. "She keeps wandering off like that and you're in big trouble."

"Keep her on the lead, Addams," someone else called out.

Smith leaned out of his cubicle and ruffled the platinum hair on his kid. "Seriously, man, you should spring for a newer model. They're expensive but the reduced mental faculties help keep them from wandering off. And they don't need to eat as much."

"We didn't all get that fat Christmas bonus, Smith." Addams made his way back to his desk, dragging the girl by the arm and wiping the sweat from his brow with a handkerchief.

I looked down at my kid, who hadn't reacted at all to the shouting. He continued to spread crayon across the white spaces of his book. Occasionally, he would hum part of a tune that I didn't recognize.

I let go of the breath I'd been holding for Addams, glad that my kid wasn't prone to wandering. Addams wasn't the only one who couldn't afford to go private and get one of the newer models. If I'd ended up assigned a kid with a flighty temperament, I'd be stuck. Until I was dead.

I ate my usual boring lunch in the cafeteria. There wasn't much joy to be found in my flavorless cheese sandwich but at least I scored a window seat. A pleasant little park sat just across the street from the building. It was always nice to see a bit of greenery.

"Man, I would kill for some steak. Or even just ham."

Smith rolled his eyes. "Come off it, Stevenson. You've never had ham. All the ham was long gone before you were born."

"I had some of that artificial stuff once," his eyelids fluttered in pleasure at the memory. "It was divine."

"How'd you afford that?" Smith quirked an eyebrow.

"Piss off."

I ignored them. I had no interest in Smith's constant gloating or Stevenson's futile wishing. *What's the point in dreaming of something you know you'll never have?*

I glanced at my kid, checking he was still close enough. It

was something that became muscle memory pretty quickly. I used to do it with my parents' kids even when I was a child myself, long before I was ever in danger. Like I was practicing for a lifetime of paranoia.

My kid stood by the window, which was fine. That was still within a few feet of me and the others were close by anyway. I was covered by them, safe enough by association here. He stared out with those fog-colored eyes, one hand on the glass. Was he watching the children in the park below? Could he even see that far?

Stevenson glanced at him. He leaned forward and lowered his voice to a murmur. "Do you guys ever remember it?"

My eyes widened and I glanced around on his behalf. No one was close enough to hear but still, it felt like a risk just talking about it.

"Shut the hell up, Stevenson," Smith snarled, his whole demeanor changed from smug to on-edge, hackles raised like an animal under threat.

"Sometimes, I have these dreams—"

"I said shut up! Take your meds and just shut up! That's what they're for."

Stevenson looked pale and ashamed. He curled into himself and stared out of the window. If anyone noticed Smith's outburst, they didn't react. That's one thing that we've all become very good at: pretending something isn't there. Complacent and complicit.

I didn't offer any consolation to Stevenson, though a part of me wanted to. The drugs we had now were fairly recent and much more effective than those previously available. When I was young, there was nothing to keep you level, nothing to help you sleep. These days, it was only in my darkest dreams that the screams of the past crept through, ripping me awake in a sweat and leaving me sobbing in the dark. That didn't happen often.

I rid myself of the thought of it with a shake of my head, as though the heavy damp of dread could be flicked from my hair. *Thinking about it might bring it on.* Best to shut up and take your meds, as Smith said.

I scrunched up my empty lunch wrappers and stood from the table, touching my kid on the shoulder. It was time to leave.

Movement by the park caught my eye. We were too high up to read the placards but I recognized the ragged assembly of a protest when I saw it.

"CPL," I grunted. "At it again."

"Bunch of idiots. If they don't want the kids, they can give them up. See how long they last after that."

"It's not about wanting them or not," Stevenson mumbled. "It's about treating them better."

"Shut it, Stevenson," Smith spat. "They don't care how they're treated." He shook his kid roughly by the shoulders to prove his point.

The boy with the platinum hair didn't flinch. He just looked dreamily around the room with his empty face.

I, on the other hand, winced. I did nothing more about it, though. Complacent and complicit. *The kids aren't real people. They're a bulletproof vest. Don't get attached. When they grow too old and their eyes clear, you'll trade them in anyway.*

We didn't know what happened to the older ones. It was safer not to ask. I looked down at the protesters again. I understood their cause but I could see no way for change. How do you challenge a system when it's all that's keeping you alive? Did that make me a bad person? Yes, it probably did, but years of medicated apathy had numbed me almost to the core.

The protest was still going when I left work.

I drowned out the chanting and the sign-waving with music from my headphones and averted my eyes. Most others were doing the same but some had gathered to smirk and mock. Police rallied, their kids dressed in bulletproof gear. Oversized helmets made them look even younger, wobbling around in that top-heavy way toddlers do, staying behind their assigned officer at all times. Better the cop took the bullet, if there was one. More chance of survival from getting shot than from losing your kid.

Shame gnawed at the edge of my numbness and I gritted my teeth. *Get home, get a drink, take your meds. You're doing too much thinking.*

I was so focused on not looking at the protestors, I stepped out to cross the street blindly, guiding my kid by the shoulder.

Tires screeched.

The driver swerved and corrected in time to avoid us. The one next to him didn't. I threw myself aside, rolling across the ground as he bounced off the first car and flipped up onto the curb. The pedestrians didn't have time to run. My head cradled in my arms, I looked up in time to see a rolling mass of metal flatten them.

My heart pounded in my ears. My vision blurred and my breath roared inside me. I checked myself. No wounds, nothing beyond scrapes from my dive.

Someone was screaming.

Head bleary with shock, I looked for the source. One guy had hurled himself frantically out of the way but the wreckage still trapped his leg. He screamed and screamed, alternating between clutching at the wound and beating his fists against the ground in mindless agony. There was so much blood.

I stood, legs shaking, and reached out as though there was anything I could do to help him.

"My kid," he screamed suddenly, thrashing left and right to look around, pinned by the wreck like a bug to a bit of cardboard.

I froze.

A child's shoe lay in the path of the car. A little black size five death-sentence, already growing cold.

The man grew frantic, writhing to get free and howling as he wrenched at his trapped leg.

Under my breath, I started to count.

"Help me!" The flesh of his leg tore as he struggled for his life. "Help me! Help me!"

When I got to seven, a snarl ripped the air, a ragged noise from a predator's throat. In the same second, invisible teeth pierced both sides of the man's neck. His screams turned to gurgles and stopped altogether as his head was severed completely.

I couldn't see the thing, blood didn't even stain its teeth. I could only hear it chewing.

A moment later, the rest of the body was wrenched sideways hard enough to free it from the wreckage. Powerful limbs lifted it high and carried it up the side of the building as though it weighed no more than a straw man.

I let go of a breath I didn't realize I'd been holding. It was over. I hadn't seen anyone killed by one of them in a long time. I heard a snuffling breath somewhere behind me, somewhere close.

Oh god, where was my kid? I'd been so caught up in the accident I forgot to look, to even think. I'd just barely seen the wreck coming in time to throw myself aside. He couldn't have seen anything at all.

His body lay some fifteen feet away. From where I was, I saw one of his legs was twisted up, joints bent in ways they shouldn't be. His blood was dark where it pooled on the road. He was very still.

My heart froze. My kid was gone. Dead. I had seconds to live and I filled them with petrified inaction.

Footsteps sounded behind me. It was going to hurt, I knew that much. They always tore prey limb from limb. Sometimes they carried people off and ate them alive.

"Sir, stay still! Don't move!"

The police. They came running over from the protest. Three of them went to check the wreck while a handful formed a ring around me, backs to me, their kids between me and the outside world.

I couldn't breathe. Small lights flashed in my eyes. I sank to my knees.

"Take the kid's hand, sir," one of the officers shouted

over his shoulder, his pointless gun raised and tracking things he couldn't see. "Take the hand. It'll be okay, we've got you!"

The hand was small and cold in mine. I followed the arm up to the kid's face. A girl. She looked right at me. Was that loathing in her eyes? Pity? Judgment? Or nothing at all?

<hr>

The hospital had its own kids, stationed on every ward, but I still didn't feel safe.

How close had I been to death? Had one of them snuck just inches behind me? Had they been reaching out with claws and teeth and tentacles? I'd never know. I couldn't stop thinking about it and every few seconds I shuddered with the horror of it.

"Just some shock, minor scrapes and bumps. You were very lucky."

I didn't feel lucky. I felt cold and hot and sick. I curled up into my chair in the waiting room. The kid here was one of the new ones—platinum hair and a mindless expression, staring straight ahead like a doll. I kept checking to see if he was looking at me. Did he know? Did he know I'd gotten mine killed?

"Sign here, here, and here. Our system shows that your insurance will cover this visit, but your extended stay here is going to cost extra. I'm afraid your coverage doesn't include an Intermediary Period."

"Intermediary...?" The words came through a fog. "What do you mean 'days waiting here'? Waiting for what?"

"Your replacement kid. I assume you're on the government standard. File says that's what you had before. A new one will take a few days to arrive. Unless you can afford to buy private or stay with someone, although I can't recommend the latter. Sharing a kid isn't a good idea. All it takes is one absentminded trip to the bathroom, just a couple of steps out of range—"

"I have to wait here?"

"You don't have to, but the hospital accepts no responsibility for your safety if you leave the site without a kid."

"How much does it cost to wait?"

"$4500 per day. That includes two meals since you won't be able to leave to buy your own food. New kids usually arrive within five days."

My head throbbed and I was suddenly exhausted. Dealing with the facts and figures of reality bled the shock out of me, but fatigue took its place.

"I can't afford that," I mumbled, mostly to myself. What the hell was I going to do?

"There are payment plans. Why don't we discuss it tomorrow? I can see you're still in shock and your insurance covers you for one night anyway."

The waiting area was full of desolate people like me. Kidless and hopeless.

We were a paranoid bunch, jittery like addicts without a fix; pacing about, jiggling limbs, casting furtive glances around for things we'd never see coming.

They placed more kids in this part of the building, I guess because we were the only ones who didn't have our own. Every time I looked at one of them, I saw that mangled body, the right leg all wrong. I felt sick.

Beds were available but I couldn't imagine sleeping like this, with no kid in his cot beside me. I hadn't slept alone in a room since I was a child. Every time I closed my eyes, I heard those footsteps behind me; and every time, they grew louder and heavier. Flashes of childhood memories crept through the cracks in my mind. Something sinewy and scaled crawled across a ceiling. A huge rounded skull, pitted with dozens of dark holes in which hungry eyes glinted, face pressed against my window. Its breath fogged up the glass but my parents couldn't see it.

Christ, I needed my meds. My stash was at home. Asking for more here was just going to increase my bill. I got up and went to the coffee machine. At least that was free.

"Hey, buddy."

An orderly, I think. Not a doctor or a nurse anyway—

wrong color clothes. *Scrubs, that's what they call them.* I stared at him blankly.

"Tough break waiting on a government replacement, huh?" He glanced around for anyone who might be listening. "This is the most expensive hotel in town and the food still sucks." He laughed at his own joke, a throaty sound that smelled like nicotine. "I might have another option for you, if you don't feel like being charged an arm and a leg for the privilege of being unlucky."

I frowned. I couldn't afford the bill, I knew that much. Come morning, I'd be forced to either incur debts that I could never hope to pay or step outside without protection and get ripped apart before I made it six paces.

For a moment, I was right back there on the road, hearing footsteps behind me. I could've sworn there was a whisper of breath in my ear.

I shook it off.

"I'm listening," I said. "What do you suggest?"

There were six kids in the back of the van. They wore the standard grays that all kids wore, white eyes blinking out at us.

"Older models," the orderly explained. "Not too old, mind you. Good for a couple of years before their eyes clear. I got all their papers so it'll all look official."

The kids made no move when the van door opened, save to turn and look out. They sat still even now, just watching. I stayed close to the orderly's kid on the walk down through the building and out the side door. Even now, I felt exposed, like I was naked in a fathomless ocean, darkness and teeth below just waiting to consume me. This was a van of lifelines.

"How much?"

"$400," he said. "A lot cheaper than staying here."

I gritted my teeth. $400 was still a lot, but it was better than being ripped apart on the street. I nodded.

The orderly grinned and dragged the nearest kid out of the van. "Here you go."

The kid was taller than my last by at least a head. "Isn't he a little old?"

"Just a growth spurt. Call it a defect with some of these older ones. He's only ten, got at least two years of sight left in him."

"What about one of the others?" I looked into the van. Five pairs of milky eyes stared back at me.

"You take what you're given, man." The smile was gone from the orderly's face. His shoulders squared. "Get the fuck out of here before I change my mind."

I couldn't argue. I needed a kid. The paranoia was chewing on my nerves, fraying my mind. It was like constantly dangling over a precipice, never knowing if the rope would break. I placed a hand on the kid's shoulder and we left.

My hand was still there after an hour of walking. I couldn't stomach the idea of letting go but I was starting to relax now that I had a kid again, starting to take back control over my mind. I still had to remind myself to take deep breaths. Once I locked myself inside the house and took my meds, it would all be fine. I repeated this like some sacred mantra to ward off insanity.

I didn't have any money left after buying the kid, which is why we were walking. It was going to be a tight few weeks until payday. I hoped the kid didn't eat much. The older versions were closer to actual children. I remembered eating at the kitchen table with the pair my parents had. I'd watch them with distrust as I ate my cereal. They ate their nutrient paste without complaint, and sat in their matching gray overalls.

Looking back, I could see how much more alert they were than the kids these days. They weren't so different from me, except for their milky eyes and the strange silence they sat in.

I frowned at my own train of thought. I wasn't supposed to feel any kind of pity. They weren't human, not really. They were tools, instruments, a bulletproof vest to protect against a hidden gunman. That's how it had to be.

I pictured my last kid again, mangled by the accident. Under my hand, the shoulder of the new kid was cold.

"Is it far?"

I flinched at his question. They normally only spoke when spoken to. "What? My place? Still another twenty minutes at least."

He was looking around a lot, tracing the movement of unseen things across rooftops and in alleyways. "There are a lot of them," he said.

My throat went dry. "More than usual?"

"Yes."

Perhaps some other unfortunate soul had lost his kid and they were flocking to the grisly scene for whatever scraps were left. I prayed for the misfortune of others and ignored the guilt washing over me.

"They're following us."

I picked up the pace, practically pushing the kid along ahead of me. My heart hammered in my eyes. My vision blurred and my breath roared inside me. The pre-dawn streets were empty. There was no help, no bolt-hole. Home was the only option.

"Almost there," I said, mostly to myself.

The kid veered from the pavement suddenly and I almost lost my grip on him.

My voice went shrill with panic. "What are you doing?!"

"They're blocking the pavement. We have to go around."

"Christ, warn me next time! I almost let go!"

The kid weaved his way up the street, moving around things that I couldn't see, things I didn't want to see. I kept a tight grip on him. I knew they couldn't touch me unless I was out of his range. They were ghosts to me. Still, I was terrified.

Finally, the kid came to a stop.

"What are you doing? Let's get moving!"

"I can't. They've cut us off."

My insides filled with the liquid cement of dread, quickly hardening. This wasn't right. They didn't behave like this. So long as you were with a kid, they paid you no attention. This couldn't be happening.

"Oh," said the kid. He tilted his head, shook himself, and tilted the other way. My knuckles were white on his shoulders.

"What? What is it?!"

"I can't see them anymore."

He turned to me. His eyes were a deep brown.

My heart stopped dead in my chest.

Hot breath washed over my neck, carried on a deep, hungry growl.

EPIPHANY

I stumble as I am pushed into the new room.

The hood is ripped from my head and the door slams before I can turn around. I wasn't going to bother anyway. There's no fighting back. Pleas for food or water fall on deaf ears. I can't remember the last time I ate.

My eyes stream in the daylight. The last room was entirely dark; so perfectly black that I lost myself in it. I had no way to track the number of days I was in there. It might have been a few. It might have been a month.

No, not as much as a month. Use your head. There was no food or water. A month of that would have left you dead. You haven't bled yet either. It can't have been more than two weeks.

I take deep breaths and try to open my eyes again. Even the pallid light of the overcast day brings them slamming shut in searing pain. I catch only a glimpse of the room. There's a wide opening in one wall, the floor sloping towards it. That explains the bitter cold at least. I am exposed to the whims of the mountain here.

Inching carefully back to the door, I ease myself onto the ground and hug my knees. In the dark room I had cautiously felt my way around, checking every corner, every inch of floor. I dare not do that here with the precarious opening and the slanted floor. My only option is to force my eyes to bear the light. If I can see, I can plan. I can look for a way out. I can hope.

It's taken hours for my eyes to adjust and, even now, they stream every second I keep them open.

The room is as plain as I expected. No furniture, no decoration. Comfort is the precise opposite of the purpose here, after all. None of the rooms so far have contained anything that could be used to escape. I'm not even able to pry free a stone from the wall that I might use to break through the door or bludgeon one of my captors.

At least the view is spectacular. Snowy, jagged peaks as far as the eye can see. No hope of signaling for help; the Tower of Arts is isolated geographically and politically. Even if I could find a way to make such a signal, no one would respond. The Tower is the forge of creation. Who would argue with that? Who could dream of challenging the birthplace of the Great Works?

It was an honor to be invited here.

I snarl and try to spit into the corner, but my mouth is too dry. My lips sting with dehydration.

The floor is so severely sloped that I have to constantly fight to keep from sliding toward the edge.

Always, I am off-balance. Always, I must keep myself tense against gravity. Sleep is impossible, and every time I drop off, I slide towards oblivion.

The cold gnaws at me constantly, and frost often forms on the stone, making movement all the more precarious. I feel safest in one of the corners, where I grip the rough brick of the walls until my fingers are numb, and then jam my hands into the crease behind my knees to try and warm them again, relying on my heels to prevent me from sliding.

I bear a thin shift and no shoes. Such luxuries as proper clothing and footwear were some of the first things stripped from us on arrival. Then, it had been under the guise of making ourselves pure, shutting out all distractions of extravagance. It was exciting. It was almost a holy endeavor. The novices gathered in the hall had been enlivened at the prospect. They had traveled far and wide to take a coveted spot at the Tower of Arts; this was the first step on their journey to a Great Work of their own.

I wonder how many of them are still alive.

Thanks to the missing wall, I am free to watch the sun sail across the sky. Some days, it seems to do that faster than others.

My fingers and toes become red and sore, then white and numb. I can't feel them anymore no matter how much I rub them or breathe on them. Even my breath seems cold, as though there's no warmth left in me. My ears sting, at least for the first day or so. After that, they, too, are numbed. I know the cold will kill me if I don't fight it. I have to keep fighting.

They don't feed me. Hunger gnaws at my guts and consumes my thoughts. A bird lands at the edge of the hole, and I nearly lunge at it, ready to tear it apart and consume it raw. I stop myself. It is too dangerous to try and catch it at the edge, and I don't think I could bring myself to kill it in any case, much less eat it. I've never killed a living thing.

I have access to water, at least. There is enough heat left in my body to melt the frost that forms on the walls, and I suck it down with bloody lips. It is never enough. The biggest clumps of frost form at the edge of the hole, and, time and time again, I am drawn to them. Gripping the wall with fingers I cannot feel and sliding on the sloped ground with legs that shake from weakness, I am torn between thirst and safety. Each time I manage to drink from these dangerous oases and make it back to the corner, I tell myself I will not risk it again. Each time the thirst becomes too much, I do it anyway.

The lack of sleep is worse than hunger or thirst. I am constantly dizzy. The sky outside swims, and the mountain peaks sway in the howling wind.

I jolt awake. Beetles are poured on me, stinging me, biting my skin. I cry out and slap at them desperately, but they vanish. Perhaps they were never there.

I hear my father's voice sometimes. *"Sonia, my little love, I knew you could do it. I knew you had the talent. I'm so proud of you. My wonderful girl, you will never have to worry about money or food again—none of us will!"*

I can almost see him, unable to keep still from the excitement, beaming with pride.

My toes turn black. My fingers are spared only by keeping them in my armpits. Doing so makes me far less safe from the terrible slant of the floor, but a part of me still clings to the hope that I might use them to get out of this. Maybe I can break free when they're moving me to the next room. Maybe I can lure one of them in and push them out of the hole. I shudder at the thought of killing someone. Even after all they've done to me…

I've lost track of the days. Someone screams from one of the other rooms, and I want to reach towards the sound, to reach out with comfort, to help, to just be near a person again. To be with someone who understands.

Each room is the worst until you're brought to the next. Each level of suffering is an escalation from the last.

"Some of you," the Maestro addressed us in the entrance hall, "have Great Works inside you. The things you experience here will draw them out. Only through the most extreme of experiences can we transcend the cage of the physical and find true epiphany! Through this process, you will be forever changed. This is our promise to you."

We whispered and tittered at this. A Great Work? From us? It seemed like something we could scarcely dare to dream of. *Forever changed* did not seem like a threat then.

I realize the one screaming is me.

I'm in my room above my father's shop.

The rain makes two sounds—a patter on the roof and a drumming in the bucket beneath the hole. It's so cold. I gave my blanket to Harlan to comfort him through the fever. I know it's selfish, but I wish I hadn't. I can't feel my fingers. How am I supposed to work this way?

I am tired to the bone, and hunger gnaws at me. I stare at the ceiling and wonder how long I can go on like this.

I think about running away. I've thought about it often these last few years. The heavy old wood of the shop forms a box that traps me, and my family takes all the air inside. I do everything I can to support my father, trying to ignore the fact that his failing eyesight means that, soon, I will need to do even more.

I could slip out into the night. I could lose myself anywhere in the empire. But then what would they do? Without me, they would be so much worse off. How could I do that to them?

If I don't, my future will be the same as my present—a lifetime of giving everything and receiving nothing.

Pain lances through my feet. I try to curl into myself, to draw myself away from the hurt, but I can't move my arms or legs.

I look down. My father is at the foot of the bed. His eyes glow, and his face is coated in frost. He takes my blackened toes into his mouth and begins to chew.

I scream myself awake, thrashing against straps that bind me to the floor.

A slap stops my panic, stinging my cheek and resetting my senses. The room is white. I am tied down. There are two people here, one in a doctor's mask, the other wearing the robes of a Maestro, black and gold. Those are the colors of a master metalsmith.

"Hold still," the voice from behind the mask advises. "This will be easier for you if you do."

I look down and meet his dark lenses. I can't see the eyes behind them. He holds a tool not unlike a pair of pruning shears in his gloved hand. Several of my toes are gone already.

"The frostbite was too severe. I'm sorry."

"Do not apologize, doctor!" The Maestro's voice is deep and smooth, and his tone suggests amusement. "This young novice is here precisely for this very reason. Change is pain, and pain is change. Only through suffering can we be set free and allowed to soar to new heights of creativity!"

The doctor does not respond. The Maestro tilts his head to regard me for a moment. There's no hint of mercy in those eyes. He seems jolly. "The only true paint is blood, little sister. The only true medium is trauma. Continue the procedure, doctor."

I scream until I pass out.

When I awaken, the straps are undone, and my toes are gone. My feet are wrapped in bandages stained pink. Pain drives needles up my legs, and every movement seems to make it worse.

I am still in the white room and the Maestro is there, watching me. A bowl of food is between us. Some kind of oat gruel. The smell of it drives my stomach wild.

"Eat." The Maestro smiles. "You must be hungry."

I throw myself onto the bowl before he finishes talking, my body acting on its own.

"You were smart to save your fingers." He pats my head while I bury my face in the food. "Losing them would be quite the blow to a seamstress, I think. The great Maestress Sindra lost most of hers but learned to play with her feet.

Have you heard her music? It never fails to move one to tears. Truly a Great Work."

My stomach roils and aches, curling me into a ball. The gruel hurts my throat and leaves a tangy taste on my tongue.

"We'll have a Great Work out of you too. Otherwise, what use are you?"

I throw up twice in the corner.

Empty again, I tremble. My stomach clenches hard, folding me in half. Despite the stress and the lack of food, the cramps have come at last.

My blood stains the white floor as the room starts to spin. The red seems bright against the white. As I watch, it grows, not outward across the ground but upwards into the air. My breath quickens. It's too hot. The blood forms a tower whose shape I recognize from the long journey through the snowy mountain passes. A tower of agony. I stand atop it, at the highest point in the empire, as close to heaven as possible, but all I want to do is jump.

Instead, I shake off the mad image and crawl over to eat my own vomit. Who knows when they'll feed me again?

Each day, I am offered the same meal of gruel. I assume it's daily—I have no way of knowing. Each time they bring it, I try to resist eating but am forced by the whip of hunger to obey. Each time I do, the hallucinations come again, then the vomiting. Nobody cleans up the mess. Nobody cleans up my blood. I am forced to relieve myself in the corner, and that isn't cleaned either. I am coated in filth and too exhausted to care. I feel thin, stretched out, worn away, far more than I ever did at night in the room above my father's shop.

"Why?!" I scream at the Maestro.

"Why?" He seems confused by the question. "For art, of course! I saw the dress you made for the countess. Resplendent. You have the talent. You must transcend if you are ever to create a Great Work."

"I am a seamstress! How will I create here?! I have no needles, no thread, no cloth!"

"Ah; this room is not for creation of the physical. Here is where you create your mind. These white walls are your canvas. Use them to see into yourself. Create yourself. Experience epiphany."

After he leaves, the walls melt into dozens of mouths, and they all scream.

I fall through time.

Reality changes with every heartbeat. There's nothing solid to grasp, nothing to hold onto.

I hear beautiful singing from somewhere outside the room. There is a commotion and shouts of, "Epiphany! Transcendence!"

The door opens and the Maestro walks in. His boot catches me across the face before I can rise.

"Worthless," he spits as I add more blood to the floor. "You hold yourself back!"

When I look again, he's gone. My mouth is bleeding, and a tooth comes free in my fingers.

Screams echo around the room. I don't know if they're mine.

The door opens and a body is thrown in. It's a young man. His head has been shaved, and his lips and nose are gone. His naked body is coated in bruises and burn marks. He leaps onto all fours and snarls at me, eyes bright with frenzy. I know he will try to kill me.

He lunges, and we go rolling. I thought I would just let it happen, but instead, I fought him. My instincts, at least, are determined that I should live.

His teeth tear into my shoulder, and I yelp. Our tumble ends with me on top. Both of us are weak and desperate. My thumbs find his eyes, and I press as hard as I can. We scream together.

I keep hitting his head against the floor again and again, long after he has stopped twitching, and then I retreat into a corner and sob until I pass out.

No meal has been brought to me for days. My stomach folds itself smaller and smaller as my hunger grows.

The body is still there. I know what I must do.

My mind goes far away as I break bones and tear flesh, forcing it down my throat. There's so little left of me now. I am a ragged, filthy, broken thing. My hair comes out in clumps and there are sores on my scalp. My family wouldn't recognize me. It's their fault I'm here.

Everything that was me has been annihilated, and in my place, this filthy creature eats the dead.

The body is gone when I wake up. There's no blood. I don't know if it was real, but it doesn't matter anymore.

I wake up again, and I am bound to a chair by my wrists and ankles.

The chair is rigid. It forces my back into an uncomfortable position.

Two Maestros are with me. I recognize neither. One wears green and bronze—a poet. The other deep blue and silver. I'm not sure what that one is. I can't remember and it doesn't seem important.

"No epiphany yet, sister. Not to worry. We are here to help."

They have a tray of sharp implements. Some curved, some straight—all gleaming and wicked.

I think I'll be too numb to feel the cutting; there's not enough of me left to react to the pain.

I'm wrong.

The pain pierces deep enough to reach me no matter how far into myself I retreat. There's nowhere to hide from it in that chair. I scream and scream.

When they're done, the doctor stitches me back together again.

I can't tell if it's the same one as before or not. The Tower must have more than one, given the amount of novices they take on. There must have been fifty of us in that hall. I wonder how many are still alive. I wonder if any of them had their epiphany. I'll never know. I'm going to die here, of that I'm sure. It's only a question of when. I can't create a Great Work. There's nothing left inside me.

The Maestros weren't trying to kill me, and the doctor did good work. Their aim is pain, not death. I'm patched up. I'll heal. They'll do it all again. Who knows how long for? Who knows what rooms come after this one?

I just wanted to get away from my family, from the weight of them. Was that so bad? Do I deserve this?

No. No one deserves this. Somehow, impossibly, I find a spark inside myself. Not creativity, not epiphany, but hatred. Rage.

Day after day they carve their way into me.

My body is a wreck, held together by stitches. I would

make an ugly dress. The thought makes me laugh between screams.

The pain no longer drains me. They're not taking things away with each cut anymore. Instead, every new torture adds to that spark of loathing. The fire grows day by day. I'm not going to die yet, I know that with certainty. There's something I want to do before I leave this body behind and go on to whatever's next.

Leaving me in the chair between sessions is a mistake. It gives me plenty of time to work on the straps. Whenever I'm left alone, I wriggle against them until my legs and shoulders burn. The stitchwork on them is inferior and the irony isn't lost on me that my superior sewing put me here and someone else's poor work will release me. Bit by bit, the straps loosen.

The Maestros never check them. Complacent in their total power over me, they go merrily about their business, often stopping to discuss the latest Great Work while I quietly bleed. They don't notice I'm free until I've stepped from the chair and grabbed the sharpest tool I can find.

That first step betrays me. It's been so long since I've stood up that my legs shake uncontrollably. My lunge becomes a fall, and I collapse onto the poet. His cry is cut short as I bury the tool in the side of his neck, and we both go down. I am trapped beneath his weight as the other runs to the door. Desperately, I try to shift the dying body, but I have grown so weak, and the strength of hatred only takes me so far.

I can't let the other one get away. I need more time before the alarm is raised. My arms shake as I heave against the body and inch by inch, I roll it off me. I am exhausted by the effort, panting and bloody, still bleeding from today's cuts and drenched by the open wound of the Maestro I killed.

Too slow. I know I've been too slow. The other one has

had more than enough time to get the door open and get away.

Instead, he is pressed against it, staring at me in horror.

Confused, I look down at the body. The door is locked, I realize. This one had the keys.

I look back to the trapped Maestro and start to laugh.

I don't feel bad about killing the doctor.

He shows up and bangs on the door at the same time as always. I drag him inside and stab him before he knows what's going on. I need his needle and thread. Catgut. Very fine. Not the material I'm used to, but it will do. The Maestros were kind enough to provide precision tools that work very well for my purpose.

It's a long time before anyone comes to look for the doctor. He's normally with me for several hours a day.

I push myself hard, through pain, through gritted teeth and numb fingers. Hatred keeps me going.

By the time they start banging on the door, I'm almost done.

By the time they find a spare key and get it open, I've put the dress on and laid open my wrists. I won't give them the satisfaction of killing me. I'll take myself out of this hell.

My vision is tunneling from blood loss. Their shapes are indistinct. I can't see their faces.

"The only true paint is blood," I tell them. "The only true medium is trauma."

As I slump sideways and let myself drift away, I hear applause.

I wake slowly.

Pain, that constant companion, has been reduced to a dull throb. My head feels packed with cotton wool.

I am somewhere soft. The sensation has become so foreign to me that I almost don't recognize it. I am on a bed.

Frowning through the muggy clouds, I search for anything that might make sense. My wounds are stitched and cleaned. In fact, my body is clean. The filth has been scrubbed from my skin. My nails have grown and been trimmed, removing any sign of the chipped talons that were there before. Slowly, my limbs obeying me only in loose terms, I reach up to my head. My hair has been growing back.

The room is unlike anything I have seen before in the Tower but I know in my bones I am still here. I haven't escaped. They've kept me alive. In spite of everything, they've kept me alive and it's going to keep going. I was stupid to think they'd let me go that easily.

I am filled with a sudden wild energy, a need to get out. I'm alone in the room. If I can act quickly, if I can go for the throat this time, maybe I'll be beyond saving.

My legs won't obey me. They are too clumsy and the blankets are too heavy.

I glance around wildly for anything that I might use but there's nothing. The room is clean and spartan. There is a window hidden behind thick curtains. Perhaps I can jump.

The door opens and a doctor comes in with a Maestro in white alongside him. A knife-master, an artist of the scalpel and the syringe.

"Ah!" The Maestro claps his hands in delight. He's missing three of his fingers and one of his ears. "You're awake! And just in time too! How wonderful!"

"Where? How?" My throat is dry and those are the only words I can manage.

The doctor comes forward with water. "Drink slowly."

"You're in the Tower, of course!" The Maestro's demeanor is every bit as bright and pleasant as the others were while they cut me. Hatred raises its ugly head again. I want to stab him. I want to strangle him until his eyes bulge and his tongue turns black.

"You belong to us now, sister." He smiles. "We're your family. We'll always be here."

Family. A word that means things to me he couldn't possibly understand. A term that comes with a weight of inevitability that hangs around the neck until it breaks the spine of you.

"And, as I said, you're just in time."

He moves to the curtains and throws them open. The window beyond looks down into the Tower to a vast hall below. All the Great Works are there. Maestress Vinner's sculpture *The Rise of the Empire* looms over all, a gargantuan work of pristine marble. Maestro Emilio's *Triumph at Dawn* hangs on the wall in a gilded frame. Through the glass, I hear the divine music of Maestress Sindra playing. There are dozens of Great Works on display for the crowd of Maestros. They gather before a new item, hidden beneath a royal red sheet.

"No," I whisper, my eyes burning with tears.

The sheets are pulled aside.

Within a glass display case, my dress hangs on a frame. A ball gown of human skin, daubed with blood and sequined with teeth ripped from the mouths of Maestros. The crowd gasps and claps, clearly delighted.

"Transcendent." The Maestro speaks in hushed, awed tones. "The flesh itself as art. You have opened new doors for us all, sister. A new age of pushing the boundaries of creativity. A true epiphany."

The applause is thunder in my ears and the sky falls around me.

ACKNOWLEDGMENTS

There are so many people that I am thankful for. If I were to try and name them all, it'd probably fill a book of its own.

Firstly, all the people at Quill & Crow who brought this project to life. Cassandra, for giving me the opportunity to share these stories with you. Fay Lane, for creating the gorgeous cover. Damon, for helping me make them the best they could be.

I am also endlessly grateful to my partner, who listens to my rambling ideas, asks questions, and engages with me on these weird mental jaunts that become stories. No matter how creeped out she gets.

But the most thanks is owed to my fellow members of The Trenches writing group. Through countless rejections, personal strife, and complications, they've never failed to be there with support, encouragement, and the odd kick in the pants (or appropriate hex) where needed. I love you guys.

ABOUT THE AUTHOR

Jim is a lover of all things dark and weird. He was raised in a Victorian-era asylum and ghosts have followed him since. He's had short stories published with the likes of Flame Tree Press, The NoSleep Podcast, Crystal Lake Publishing, Eerie River Publishing, and many others. Jim is a comic book nerd, a Dungeon Master and a cryptid enthusiast. He doesn't trust trees and he doesn't think you should either.

TRIGGER INDEX

THANK YOU FOR READING

Thank you for reading *Change & Other Terrors*. We deeply appreciate our readers, and are grateful for everyone who takes the time to leave us a review. If you're interested, please visit our website to find review links. Your reviews help small presses and indie authors thrive, and we appreciate your support.

Other Crow Collections

#1 - Ending in Ashes, Rebecca Jones Howe

#2 - My Little Black Book of Horror, Cassandra L. Thompson

#4 - Bury Me Cold & Other Last Words, Jacob Steven Mohr

www.ingramcontent.com/pod-product-compliance
Lightning Source LLC
Chambersburg PA
CBHW031751200726
48289CB00013B/785